Running for their lives . . .

"Louis!" Jessica cried, throwing her arms around him. "I don't want to go. You just had a dream, Louis. A dream." A sob rose in her throat. She couldn't face getting in the car and running again. Here in the mountains, she felt as if they had found a kind of magic circle in which they were safe from Chloe. "Please don't make me leave today," she murmured, pressing her cheek against his flannel shirt.

She could hear his heart beating hard inside his chest. Slowly it resumed its normal rhythm. Louis put his arms around her waist and squeezed. "All right," he agreed. "But tomorrow morning we have to go. No arguments."

Jessica nodded mutely. The truth was that she and Louis would never be safe. Because Chloe would hunt them to the ends of the earth—and until the end of time.

Bantam Books in the Sweet Valley University series
Ask your bookseller for the books you have missed

And don't miss these
Sweet Valley University Thriller Editions:

SWEET VALLEY UNIVERSITY®

Deadly Attraction

Written by
Laurie John

Created by
FRANCINE PASCAL

BANTAM BOOKS
NEW YORK · TORONTO · LONDON · SYDNEY · AUCKLAND

RL 6, age 12 and up

DEADLY ATTRACTION

A Bantam Book / December 1995

Sweet Valley High® and Sweet Valley University®
are registered trademarks of Francine Pascal
Conceived by Francine Pascal
Produced by Daniel Weiss Associates, Inc.
33 West 17th Street
New York, NY 10011

ISBN: 0-553-56698-9

Published simultaneously in the United States and Canada

Bantam Books are published by Bantam Books, a division of Bantam
Doubleday Dell Publishing Group, Inc. Its trademark, consisting of the
words "Bantam Books" and the portrayal of a rooster, is Registered in
U.S. Patent and Trademark Office and in other countries. Marca
Registrada. Bantam Books, 1540 Broadway, New York, New York 10036.

PRINTED IN THE UNITED STATES OF AMERICA

OPM   0 9 8 7 6 5 4 3 2 1

To Erica Brooke Carson

Chapter One

Elizabeth Wakefield glared at her identical twin sister. "Care to explain these?" she asked, removing a stack of eight-by-ten black-and-white photos from the envelope in her hand. She hurled the pictures at Jessica's back, and they scattered across her sister's red, blue, and yellow quilt.

Elizabeth had just walked into the dorm room she shared with her twin. She'd found Jessica lying facedown on her bed, sobbing. Usually the sight of Jessica in tears filled Elizabeth with sympathy. But at the moment she was too angry to worry about Jessica's disaster of a life. She had her own problems to think about—and Jessica was at the center of them.

Physically, Elizabeth and Jessica Wakefield were identical. Both girls had the same long, golden blond hair, blue-green eyes, and slim figures. But their personalities were vastly different.

Although she was only a freshman, Elizabeth was a serious student. She had distinguished herself both academically and as a broadcast journalist prepared to expose corruption wherever she found it.

So far, Jessica had devoted her freshman year to her sorority, parties, and men. In some ways, her behavior hadn't changed since high school. She had been wild and impulsive then. And she was wild and impulsive now.

Once again, Jessica had gotten herself into a huge mess that had not only backfired on her but on Elizabeth as well. And this time, the mess had been captured on film.

Jessica sat up, brushing tears from her cheeks. "What are these?" she asked, reaching for a photo.

Elizabeth put her hands on her hips. "Smile. You were on *Candid Camera*."

Jessica's mouth dropped open as she looked at the picture in her hand. "Oh, no!" she screamed.

"Funny, that's exactly what I said." Elizabeth's tone was caustic, but Jessica seemed too distracted by the photos that surrounded her to respond. She picked up one after the other, discarding and clutching at them in mounting panic.

The pictures were a collection of photographs featuring Jessica in the arms of Professor Louis Miles, Sweet Valley University's youngest and most handsome professor. The couple stood outside the door of what appeared to be a beach

2

condo. Jessica's hair was disheveled and their embrace was passionate.

As Elizabeth watched Jessica examine picture after picture, she reflected on the events that had led them to this sordid point. For the last several days Elizabeth and Todd Wilkins had been conducting an investigation of SVU's corrupt athletics department. It appeared that a gambling ring had been bribing certain basketball players to fix games by missing baskets, controlling the score, and manipulating the outcome.

"Point shaving," Elizabeth murmured, remembering how Todd's girlfriend, Gin-Yung Suh, had known exactly what the illegal scheme was called.

Elizabeth's investigation was making a lot of dangerous people very nervous. Todd had been attacked outside his dorm, and all indications were that the perpetrators had been somehow involved with the point-shaving ring.

So when Jessica hadn't come home the night before, Elizabeth had been worried sick. She'd stayed awake most of the night, wondering whether or not someone might have mistaken Jessica for Elizabeth. The same people who beat up Todd could have gotten to her twin. She'd been incredibly relieved when Jessica had finally come back to the dorm this morning—but she'd been irritated as well. Jessica should have called.

"When you came in this morning you said you

3

were out driving all night," Elizabeth reminded her sister. "You said you'd been upset about something that happened at Theta House."

Elizabeth paced the room, recalling Jessica's vague answers to her questions that morning. No wonder Jessica hadn't been forthcoming with information—she'd had a lot to hide.

"You *lied* to me," Elizabeth accused. "I can't believe that. You spent the night with Professor Miles, didn't you? What a stupid thing to do, Jess. What were you thinking of?"

"Where did you get these?" Jessica demanded, ignoring Elizabeth's comments. "Have you been spying on me?" Her own voice was as accusatory as Elizabeth's.

"Of course not," Elizabeth snapped. "I just left Dr. Beal's office. *He* gave them to me."

"Dr. Beal? The director of administration?" Jessica's face turned suddenly pale.

Elizabeth stamped her foot. "Yes, Jessica! Dr. Beal, the man who's the ultimate authority on this campus. Do you have any idea what this means to me?"

Jessica narrowed her eyes. "To *you*?"

Elizabeth grabbed a picture from her hands. "Yes. To me."

"What could this have to do with you? It's about me and Louis Miles. What did Dr. Beal say? Why has *he* been spying on us? What's going to happen to Louis?"

Elizabeth yanked the baseball cap she was

wearing off her head and threw it furiously against the wall. "Who cares? The man's a professor. And a professor who uses his position to seduce his students is the lowest form of sleazeball."

"Don't say that!" Jessica shouted, jumping to her feet. "It's not like that. We're in love. There's nothing sleazy about our feelings."

"No? If everything's so on the up-and-up, then why did you lie?"

Jessica blushed and turned away. "You wouldn't understand."

"Here's what I understand," Elizabeth said. "I understand that once again, you've gotten yourself involved in an inappropriate relationship. And once again, I'm the one who's paying the price. Dr. Beal just told me to drop the investigation of the athletics department."

"Or what?"

"Or he'll use those pictures to fire Professor Miles and drag you through the mud."

"But Louis can keep his job if you *do* drop the investigation?" Jessica's desperate, tearstained face turned hopeful. "He's not going to fire him?"

Elizabeth was so angry she put her hands on Jessica's shoulders and gave her a hard shake. "No. He's not going to fire him. Because I *am* going to drop the investigation. Not because I care about him, but because I care about you. No matter what, I don't want to see *you* get hurt again."

Jessica began to tremble. "Well, if it makes you feel any better, you're too late."

"What do you mean?"

"I mean, I'm already hurt. And I don't care what happens to me anymore. All I care about is Louis." She paused for a moment. "But he's married!" She wrapped her arms around herself and doubled over. Her shoulders shook and tears ran down her face.

In spite of herself, Elizabeth felt sorry for Jessica now. She really was in pain. And no matter how angry Elizabeth got with her sister, she hated to see her upset.

Elizabeth took some deep breaths to get her temper under control and then put her arm around Jessica. "Married? Are you sure?"

Jessica nodded and gulped. "I'm sure. Nobody but a wife would be so jealous she would try to kill me."

A cold dread stole over Elizabeth's limbs. "Kill you? What are you talking about?"

"When I was driving back to campus from town this afternoon, somebody followed me in a black car and bumped me a couple of times. You'd told me you were working on something to do with the athletics department, so I assumed some jock was just hassling me. But then the car tried to run me off the road. At the Pine Bluff construction site."

"Jess! Pine Bluff is an obstacle course. How did you survive it?"

Jessica groaned. "Let me put it this way, I could probably get a job as a stunt driver now."

Elizabeth smiled and handed Jessica a Kleenex from the box by the bed.

Jessica blew her nose. "Wait till you see the Jeep. It's a mess. Dad's going to have a cow."

"Never mind about the Jeep. Are you OK? No whiplash or broken bones?"

"Just a broken heart," Jessica said ruefully, squeezing her eyes shut. "When I got back to the dorm, this lady came up to me in the parking lot. She said Louis was her husband. And she said if I didn't leave him alone, I'd better be looking in my rearview mirror every single minute."

Elizabeth let out her breath with a long, weary sigh. Life was getting more complicated by the minute.

Mark Gathers walked down the long hall of the athletics complex. He'd just picked up an envelope from Dr. Beal to deliver to Coach Crane, the senior coach.

Mark knocked softly when he reached the office. Coach Crane opened the door, and Mark was surprised to Mr. Santos sitting inside. "Mr. Santos!" he said, feeling slightly alarmed. "How are you, sir?"

T. Clay Santos was the head of the SVU Alumni Association. He was a small, slightly bald, gamine man with twinkling eyes and a weather-beaten face. An easy, genial charm thinly veneered a ruthless and potentially violent personality. Right now, he didn't look pleased. Mark was a big guy, but he had to fight the urge to quail when Santos turned his blue eyes in his direction. Santos's mouth smiled, but his eyes remained hard as agates. "Hello, Mark. How's the job working out?"

"Great, Mr. Santos. Thanks," Mark answered with a respectful smile.

When someone softly cleared his throat, Mark noticed Bobbo in the corner. Bobbo nodded and gave him a faint smile. All Mark knew about the guy was that he worked for Mr. Santos, and he was huge. Basically, Bobbo looked like an ex–football player in a dark gray business suit. Mark had concluded that he was Mr. Santos's bodyguard. Next to Bobbo stood another Neanderthal-looking guy. Another bodyguard? Mark wondered if the excess of muscle indicated that Santos was expecting some kind of trouble.

Coach Crane looked tense. Mark didn't blame him. It was hard to relax with Santos around. Despite his outwardly casual manner, the man seemed as if he could explode any minute.

Coach Crane took the envelope from Mark's hand and gave it to Mr. Santos. "I've got a job for you, Mark," Coach Crane said.

"Yes, sir." Mark felt his own muscles tense.

"You know Craig Maser? The wrestler?"

"Only by sight, Coach."

"You know he's going to Las Vegas for a match with Scotty Fisher from the University of Arizona?"

Mark nodded. The event was going to air on closed-circuit broadcast through the University Broadcasting Company, a new, all-NCAA cable channel. There were posters up all over campus announcing the event. Big-screen TVs would be set up in the activities hall of the student union so that everybody on campus could watch.

"Craig's in the weight room working out. I want you go in there and get to know him. Make sure nobody talks to . . . nobody *bothers* him. OK? Todd Wilkins is in there, and you know what a pest he can be."

Mark's eyes darted back and forth between Coach Crane's strong granite face and Mr. Santos's round, smiling one. As both men stared at him, he began to understand exactly what was going on.

The outcome of the wrestling match had been arranged. Craig was being paid to take a dive. And they didn't want Wilkins or anybody else interfering with their plan.

"Sure," Mark said in a quiet voice. "I'll go right now."

Mark slipped out the door, which Coach Crane closed behind him. Alone in the hallway, Mark leaned against the wall for a minute. His palms were sweaty, and his heart was racing. He wondered if he had gotten deeper into this mess than it was safe to be.

At first glance, Santos had looked like an ordinary guy—sort of like someone's dad—in his khaki pants, loafers, and short-sleeve sport shirt. But Santos was a very scary guy. Mark had sensed his power almost immediately the night he went to see him at his huge estate, looking for a job.

Santos had told him that he would use his influence with Dr. Beal to get Mark back into school and back onto the basketball team. In the meantime, he had given Mark a fistful of money and told him he was now the official student assistant to the athletics department. The job included keeping his eyes open and reporting back to Santos if there was something he ought to know.

But Santos hadn't asked Mark to find a red Jeep and follow Elizabeth Wakefield. Mark had overheard his boss giving that job to somebody else, although he didn't know who. He'd just heard Santos giving instructions on the phone. *"There's a blond female freshman by the name of Wakefield. She drives a red Jeep. Find her and put a tail on her."*

Mark turned on his heel and headed for the weight room. He really didn't feel like dealing with Maser and Wilkins right now. But it was becoming increasingly clear that nobody said no to T. Clay Santos.

Jessica stared at the photo of herself with Louis and moaned. Elizabeth had left, saying she had to find Todd. And Jessica felt completely and utterly alone.

Had every single word that passed Louis's lips

been a lie? And if so, how could she have been so gullible?

Jessica got up and examined her reflection in the mirror. For once in her life, she wasn't concerned about her looks or her clothes. Today she'd put on the kind of straight-legged jeans that Elizabeth usually wore, along with a long-sleeve oatmeal-color T-shirt. Her hair was tangled and flat. She noticed absently that it looked like straw. But who cared?

If Louis didn't love her, nothing mattered anymore. Not her looks. Not school. Not Elizabeth's investigation. Nothing.

Love hurts. Unwillingly her brain began mentally playing the song that seemed to have become Jessica's signature tune.

So far, her college career had been one painful relationship after another. First she'd fallen hopelessly in love with Mike McAllery. They had married impulsively, but the brief union had ended in anger, recriminations, and a tragic accident. Then she'd made the mistake of getting involved with James Montgomery. She had fallen for his charm and his looks, only to discover that he was an animal. He had tried to date-rape her, and fighting back in court had been one of the hardest things she had ever had to do.

After James she'd had a short, disappointing relationship with another fabulous-looking guy named Randy Mason. Again getting caught up with his goods looks and romantic nature had blinded her to the fact that he really wasn't the right guy for her.

And now . . .

Jessica went back over to the bed and looked at another picture of herself and Louis. The image made her feel strange and a little sick. She was both ashamed and exhilarated at the sight of their intimate embrace.

Jessica and Professor Miles had fallen gradually in love over the last few weeks. They had tried to deny their feelings for each other, and at one point he had abruptly put an end to their relationship, saying it was too dangerous. A relationship with a student would endanger his job and possibly lead to a scandal for her.

At first Jessica had been heartbroken. Then she had been angry. Last night she'd gone to Louis's beach house to tell him she thought he was a hypocrite and a coward. She'd wanted the satisfaction of having the last word and walking out on *him*.

But when she arrived at his condo, their passion for each other had overridden every other concern. They had fallen into each other's arms, kissed hungrily, and lost all sense of reality for a brief few hours.

Louis was a professor. And their love was a forbidden love. When she had left this morning, he had reminded her that for now, they had to keep the relationship a secret. He had promised to work the problems out, but he needed some time.

The last thing he had said to her before she drove away was that he loved her. And that she could trust him.

How could he have lied so baldly? He *didn't* love her. And she *couldn't* trust him.

But in spite of everything, she didn't hate him. The very idea of hating him was unfathomable. He might not love her, but she still loved him. And unfortunately she didn't know how to stop.

Chapter
Two

Elizabeth strode angrily toward the athletics complex. On the way she passed an area of sidewalk under construction. There were no workmen around and the messy site was littered with trash. Elizabeth savagely kicked an empty soda can out of her path and stepped carefully over the torn-up concrete of the sidewalk.

The clattering sound of the aluminum can didn't alleviate her anger one bit, and she wished for a moment that there were a jackhammer at the site. She would take great pleasure in picking it up and dismantling the whole Sweet Valley University campus brick by brick. The school was riddled with corruption from top to bottom. Everybody seemed to be in on it—Coach Crane, the Alumni Association, and even Dr. Beal.

Earlier Todd had said he was going to the gym for a workout. Now Elizabeth needed to find him and tell him to lay off Coach Crane. Their investigation was over.

Todd wasn't going to be happy about her backing out. They had started this whole thing in an effort to get him reinstated on the basketball team. He had been suspended at the beginning of the school year for receiving special privileges.

Later, when he had applied to get his position back, his request had been turned down—despite recommendations from faculty and the team coach. Dr. Beal had told Todd that his inability to get back on the team was due to the Alumni Association's concern about the reputation of the athletics department. They didn't want anybody with a hint of scandal attached to them involved with any of the teams.

Of course, in light of what Todd and Elizabeth knew now, the association's reluctance to reinstate Todd made sense. If high-stakes gamblers were running a point-shaving operation in the athletics department—and using the athletics budget to launder the money—they would naturally want to avoid any and all scrutiny.

"Elizabeth! Elizabeth, wait!" a voice called.

She turned and saw Gin-Yung, Todd's girlfriend, running toward her. Elizabeth groaned inwardly. She knew that Gin-Yung would be full of questions, and she wasn't sure how to provide her with answers. Todd was adamant about wanting to keep Gin-Yung out of a potentially dangerous situation.

Gin-Yung caught up to Elizabeth and gasped for air. "I'm late for class," she said. "But can you tell me anything about the investigation?"

Elizabeth shook her head. "No progress."

"You're kidding," Gin-Yung said, obviously suspicious.

Elizabeth felt her face flush. She despised lying. And she considered Gin-Yung, an intelligent, fast-talking, Korean-American sports reporter for the SVU newspaper, to be a friend. Plus Gin-Yung had played a pivotal role in helping Todd and Elizabeth realize that the university administration was totally corrupt.

Gin-Yung's reporter's instincts had immediately smelled something fishy about the administration's refusal to reinstate Todd. And she'd figured out the point-shaving theory.

Todd's girlfriend had also been the one who had mentally followed the money trail to the Alumni Association and its unscrupulous head, Mr. T. Clay Santos.

Nonetheless, Todd had made Elizabeth promise she wouldn't tell Gin-Yung anything that might put her in danger. He'd been beaten up and warned off once already—he didn't want Gin-Yung taking any chances.

"You're not telling me the truth, are you?" Gin-Yung said. "You've found out something." It was a statement, not a question.

Elizabeth adjusted the bill of her baseball cap. "We've spent a lot of time tracking down players

16

who might have taken bribes from the Alumni Association. We were hoping to find one who might be willing to testify. So far, no luck."

"So? Tell me who you talked to. Anybody I suggested?" Gin-Yung looked at her expectantly.

Elizabeth hung her thumbs from the back pockets of her jeans and stared down at her toes. Gin-Yung had an encyclopedic knowledge of professional, college, and even high school sports. The data she had given them about players had been invaluable. It was only natural that she would want to know how they had used the information.

"There are problems with the investigation, and I can't talk about it yet," Elizabeth finally answered.

"Maybe I can help," Gin-Yung said.

"Nobody can help," Elizabeth said curtly.

Gin-Yung's eyebrows rose in surprise at Elizabeth's tone of voice.

"I'm sorry," Elizabeth said quickly.

Gin-Yung's face closed up a little and she took a step back. "OK, fine. Have it your way," she responded in a clipped tone. She turned and began walking rapidly away.

Elizabeth ran to catch up with her. "Gin-Yung. Gin-Yung, wait!"

Gin-Yung spun around. "Look, I'm getting the message. I've gotten it from Todd. And I'm getting it from you. You two are tight. You don't want me in the middle. Well, you can tell Todd from me that I'm out of the middle. Permanently."

"You're getting this all wrong," Elizabeth argued. "Todd and I are just friends. That's it."

"Yeah, right!" Gin-Yung said, her voice bitter.

Elizabeth and Todd had dated from the sixth grade until shortly into their freshman year of college. Now they were just friends, but it was hard for Gin-Yung to believe. Sometimes it was hard for Tom Watts, Elizabeth's own boyfriend, to believe as well.

"Look!" Elizabeth said angrily. "I can't deal with everything that's going on and jealousy, too. If you've got a problem with Todd, tell him, not me."

Gin-Yung's face was stony for a few seconds. Then she smiled reluctantly. "Hey!" she said softly. "I'm sorry. It's just that as a girlfriend *and* a reporter, I resent being pushed out of a great story—even if Todd thinks it's for my own good."

"I know you do," Elizabeth said. "That's how I felt when Tom told me to back off." *And I held my ground all the way—until now,* she thought bitterly.

Elizabeth was perfectly willing to fight Tom Watts and anybody else in the name of pursuing an important story. But she didn't want her sister's name smeared all over the campus. She didn't want Jessica's private business turned into the kind of "tabloid entertainment news" that she despised.

Elizabeth was a reporter at WSVU, the campus television station, and Tom was the general manager and head news anchor. They worked hard to keep their work professional and newsworthy, but a scandalous story like the one Dr. Beal was threatening to make public wouldn't confine itself to the SVU campus. Local news stations would love to expose an unethical professor. And there wouldn't be a thing Elizabeth could do to stop the vicious gossip.

The only way she could protect Jessica's reputation was to knuckle under to Dr. Beal's threats. Elizabeth felt her blood pressure rise as she contemplated her lack of options. The total unfairness of the situation made her furious with Dr. Beal and the entire athletics department. She was also furious with Professor Miles. And even with Jessica.

But she didn't have time to explain all that to Gin-Yung. The circumstances were too complicated. Right now, her first priority was to find Todd before he did something that might make things worse than they already were.

"*One* . . . two . . . three . . . four! *Hup* . . . two . . . three . . . four! *March* . . . two . . . three . . . four! Egbert! You're slacking. Pick up your feet!" Lieutenant Drake shouted.

Winston's legs were killing him. How long was this torture going to last? His ROTC fatigues were heavy and hot. His big combat boots weighed a ton, and the pack on his back was compressing and compacting his vertebrae with every step. He could practically feel himself shrinking.

The army was supposed to make him all that he could be. But if they didn't ease up, he was going to be less than he was when he started.

"*One* . . . two . . . three . . . four! Egbert! Stand up straighter!" The company commander's bark was low and hoarse.

When Winston tried to straighten up under the heavy pack, his rifle slipped. Then the thick, clunky toe of his boot caught on the gun's barrel and the next thing he knew, he was lying face-down on the ROTC drill field located south of the campus.

Winston watched twenty-five pairs of identical boots march past his face and disappear. "Don't bother to wait," Winston groaned sarcastically into the turf. "I'll be fine. Don't worry about me."

The grass was damp, but it felt nice and cool against his cheek.

"Company, halt!" Lieutenant Drake shouted.

With his ear to the ground, Winston could hear a muffled, percussive thump as twenty-five left feet stomped the ground, punctuating the halt. He heard another series of soft thuds as somebody backtracked in his direction. A pair of black, round toes appeared before his eyes. "Egbert!"

Winston was getting tired of being constantly addressed by his last name. Psychology 101 had taught him that one way to modify annoying behavior was for the annoy*ee* to refuse to respond to the annoy*er* in the manner anticipated. Therefore, it logically followed that if he quit answering to *Egbert,* someone would finally say *Winston,* and then he could spring to his feet and . . .

"Egbert! Get up." The booted foot nudged him rudely in his rib cage.

"I can't." Winston groaned, abandoning his attempt at behavior modification.

"Yes, you can." An enormous hand gripped his skinny upper arm and jerked upward.

"Upsy-daisy," Winston sang in a cheery falsetto, finding himself suddenly on his feet and face-to-face with a bright red Lieutenant Drake.

Lieutenant Drake commanded the respect of the men and women of his unit—not just because he was their commanding officer but also because he was an SVU senior, in superb physical condition, and the type of guy who exhibited classic leadership ability.

Winston hated him.

"What did you say?" Lieutenant Drake demanded.

"Upsy-daisy, *sir,*" Winston amended.

"Are you being funny?"

Winston studied the lieutenant's face. He wasn't laughing. And he didn't look amused. So it appeared to Winston that the question was purely rhetorical. Nonetheless, Winston had been addressed by a superior officer. Clearly some response was expected.

"Sir. No, sir," Winston responded, yelling at

the top of his voice the way he had been taught. He really couldn't fathom the military's penchant for shouting virtually *every* remark, no matter how trivial. Sure, it was probably good for the lungs. But was he being trained to fight for his country? Or sing for the Metropolitan Opera?

"Rejoin the unit," Lieutenant Drake bellowed.

"Sir. Yes, sir!" Winston yelled back. He marched toward the waiting column of fellow officers in training, lifting his knees as high as possible.

Feeling completely miserable, he thought of the cheating incident that had led him to the Reserve Officers' Training Corps in the first place. Why had he cheated on his physics test? Why? Because he was in love Denise Waters, that's why. And he'd been afraid that if he failed physics, his parents would move him to a smaller school with fewer distractions—and away from Denise.

He hadn't planned to cheat. He'd gone to the office Professor Stark shared with Professor Miles to pick up some study guides. But Professor Stark hadn't been there. When Winston searched Professor Stark's desk for the study guide, he found copies of the actual test instead. Temptation had overwhelmed him and he had grabbed one from the pile.

Naturally, he'd gotten caught.

And this was his punishment. According to his father, ROTC was going to mold his character and make a man out of him. But so far, Winston just felt humiliated. The muscles in his arms and legs shook with fatigue, and he felt close to passing out from exhaustion.

The only thing that made ROTC training close to bearable was that Denise—beautiful, wonderful, love-of-his-life Denise—had joined the ROTC too. She'd signed up as a display of solidarity. A signal of her undying affection. A token of her love.

But the light in her eyes as she watched him rejoin the unit was singularly dim. Denise was already distinguishing herself as a physical, mental, and emotional credit to her country. Winston was not. And Winston had the uncomfortable feeling that the disparity between his and Denise's military aptitudes had the potential to create a rift between them.

Chapter
Three

_____

Mark paused outside the glass door of the weight room. At first, all he saw was his own reflection—a tall guy with dark hair, wearing track shorts, a sweatshirt, and athletic shoes.

Objectively he didn't look a bit different than he had a few months ago when he had been a star on the SVU basketball team.

But Mark had aged a lifetime since then. When Elizabeth and Tom Watts had exposed the fact that certain athletes were getting unfair privileges, the athletics department had used Mark and Todd Wilkins as scapegoats. Both guys had been unceremoniously dumped from the team, and Mark had been filled with a bitter rage. He'd ended up leaving school in the middle of the night without a word to anyone—including Alexandra Rollins, who had been his girlfriend. Then he'd taken a shot at pro basketball and failed. And now he was back at SVU. But he still didn't have his old position on the team.

Right now, he was doing flunky duty for Mr. T. Clay Santos. Like Bobbo.

Mark stepped inside the hot weight room. Alex was working out in a yellow unitard. Her coppery hair was piled on top of her head and the exercise had given her a pink flush across her face and shoulders. She looked even more beautiful than she had when they'd been dating.

Her eyes met his briefly, but she didn't smile. Alex quickly averted her gaze. Mark pressed his lips together and tried to keep a lid on his anger. He had to get used to that look. His reputation had been destroyed, and so far he'd done nothing in anyone's opinion to redeem himself. For the millionth time, he wished he could turn back the clock and be a popular basketball hero again.

Mark searched the room until his eyes found Craig Maser. Sweet Valley University's star wrestler was sitting on a weight bench getting ready to do some presses with the help of Todd Wilkins.

"Let me spot for you, Craig." Mark gave Craig an ingratiating smile. "Coach Crane wants me to look after you," Mark added. "He told me to help you out."

"I don't need any help," Craig responded in a flat tone. He lay down and positioned himself underneath the bar of the weight. Todd stood behind the bench, ready to assist.

"Hey! I'm the student assistant to the athletics

25

department. So it's part of my job." Mark gave Todd a surly look. "You can get lost now, Wilkins."

Todd's face hardened and Alex, who was working on a leg flexer, gasped. She scowled at Mark. "I don't know where you've been for the last few months," she snapped. "But it obviously wasn't charm school."

Mark sneered slightly. "I'd forgotten how witty you could be, Alex." He made his voice as sarcastic as possible and Alex colored hotly.

Craig slid out from under the weight and sat up. He stared at Mark, a look of distaste on his face.

Two girls who were standing by the treadmill fell silent. And the handsome, brown-haired guy who had been talking to Alex turned his spectacled gaze in Mark's direction.

The room was now completely quiet, and Mark felt his own cheeks growing red. He knew he was coming off like a jerk.

"I don't think I want you to spot for me, Gathers," Craig said in a low voice. "When I'm lifting weights, I want to work with somebody I can trust."

Mark's red face began to burn. "What are you talking about, Maser?" he demanded in a loud voice.

"I think you know." Craig's brown eyes met Mark's and refused to look away.

Mark narrowed his eyes and leaned down so he

could speak in a whisper. "You're not any better than I am, Maser. You're on the take from Santos, and we both know it. So don't give me any . . ."

"Mark!" The sound of his name was like the crack of a whip. He straightened immediately and looked over his shoulder. Coach Crane stood in the doorway with Bobbo at his elbow. Mark felt Craig stiffen beside him. A few feet away he caught a glimpse of Wilkins's hands balling into fists.

"Is there a problem?" Coach Crane demanded.

"The problem is that Wilkins here doesn't seem to like it that I'm working for the athletics department," Mark said.

"Todd, if you have some kind of problem with Mark's position, then I suggest you direct your remarks in writing to Dr. Beal. Please refrain from harassing people in the workout room."

Todd looked at Mark, then looked at the coach and shook his head. He let out a snort of disgust and grabbed his gym bag. "I'm out of here," he said.

"I think you should consider yourself barred from the gym," Coach Crane added.

Todd laughed with disdain. He gave Coach Crane and Bobbo a long and insolent look. He walked slowly past them, watching their faces. As he neared the door, he deliberately came within inches of brushing Bobbo's shoulder. Bobbo's beefy hand flew up and grabbed a handful of Todd's T-shirt. "Watch where you step," Bobbo warned in a soft voice.

Todd gave the bodyguard an unwavering stare. "I'm too busy watching you," he replied. He pushed Bobbo's hand away and left the gym with his back straight and his head high.

Coach Crane's cold gray eyes followed Todd until he disappeared around the corner of the hallway. He jerked his head at Bobbo, and they left the gym.

When they were gone, Craig grabbed his towel and headed for the locker room. "I'm going to shower." He frowned at Mark. "And I don't need any help from you." He gave the locker room door a hard shove and walked through it, leaving it to swing back and forth with a loud squeaking sound.

Mark felt somebody watching him. When he peered around, he saw Alex frozen in midleg lift, staring at him. The guy she was with hovered protectively next to her. "What are *you* looking at?" Mark demanded, giving him a hostile look.

The guy didn't flinch at all. He just pushed his glasses up on his nose. "I'm looking at the student assistant to the athletics department," he answered in an ironic tone.

Mark turned on his heel and walked out. It wasn't any use trying to buddy up to Craig. Since Wilkins was gone, Coach Crane didn't need to worry about him bugging the wrestler.

Mark actually felt a little sick to his stomach. The last few minutes had been weird. And he hadn't exactly added any members to the Mark Gathers fan club.

Elizabeth was yards away from the front steps of the athletics complex when she spotted a familiar figure near the building's entrance. It was Dr. Beal. Tall and cadaverous, he radiated the same aura of menacing authority that he had when she'd seen him in his office. Elizabeth shuddered at the memory of him showing her the photographs and threatening to make them public if she didn't drop her investigation of the athletics department and Mr. T. Clay Santos.

Dr. Beal hurried into the front door of the athletics complex just as Todd came rushing out. They exchanged a curious look but no words.

Elizabeth stood still, digging the toe of her tennis shoe into the ground while she waited for Todd to notice her. He lifted his hand when he spotted her and hurried to her side. "Mark Gathers is all over Craig Maser," he informed her in a grim voice.

"What do you mean?" she asked.

"I think it means the fix is in on the wrestling match in Vegas."

"So it's not just basketball?"

Todd shook his head. "Basketball. Football, probably. Tennis. I guess this thing is even bigger than we thought."

"Wow! No wonder they went to so much trouble to keep us quiet." She adjusted the bill of her baseball cap to block out the sun while she explained what had happened in Dr. Beal's office.

Todd dropped his bag and sighed. "Oh, man!" he exclaimed in a voice of disbelief. "These guys are like, *evil,* and we're supposed to back off because of one of Jessica's boyfriends?"

Elizabeth's head felt as if it were going to explode. "She's my sister, Todd."

"Hey! I've known you and Jessica practically my whole life. Jessica is like a sister to me, too. But this is bigger than Jessica."

"I just can't expose Jess to the kind of publicity she's in for," Elizabeth said, her heart aching. "She's been through so much these last few months. I don't know how much more she can stand. She's at the breaking point—and I can't be the one to push her over the edge."

"You guys have got to get your act together," Mark heard Mr. Santos shouting angrily from inside Coach Crane's office. "You're losing control of this situation. And now you're telling me that someone else is setting up the Wakefield girl? Why? What's going on here?"

Mark heard buzzing voices. Dr. Beal and Coach Crane were speaking rapidly but in low tones, as if they were trying to calm Mr. Santos.

"There's a lot of serious money at stake and you guys are slipping," Santos's voice accused angrily. "You'd better not be double-crossing me . . ." His voice was drowned out by excited exclamations from Coach Crane and Dr. Beal.

Mark tiptoed across the hall and pressed his ear

against the door. Coach Crane's voice was clearly audible. "The situation is *not* out of control," Coach Crane insisted. "I don't think we should panic. Dr. Beal, tell us again where the pictures came from. There's got to be some logical explanation."

"According to my secretary, someone slipped the envelope under the door. It was marked *personal*. When I opened it and saw the pictures of the young Wakefield woman and Professor Miles, I assumed they came from you, Mr. Santos."

"I talked to my guy," Santos said. "He never located the Jeep or the girl. He never took any pictures. So if he didn't take those pictures," Santos yelled, "who did? Let me tell you guys something. The minute those kids started poking around, this whole operation started going south. Something's gotta be done. And something's gotta be done quick."

"What do you want us to do?" Dr. Beal asked.

"Nothing," Mr. Santos snapped. "I want it done right. So I'll take care of it myself."

Mark jumped backward just seconds before Santos came barreling through the door. His round face was beet red with fury. Bobbo and another sidekick followed closely behind. They left without a backward look or a word to Mark.

Mark walked over to the long window in the hall and peered out at the expanse of green grass, hedges, and intersecting sidewalks that made the athletics complex look like a collegiate haven of

31

sportsmanship. Of course, the complex was in reality a cesspool of dirty money, gamblers, corrupt school officials, and has-beens like himself.

Several yards away from the front steps, he saw Todd and Elizabeth talking intently beneath a tree. They turned and began walking in the direction of the dorms.

Todd looked as if he were trying to convince Elizabeth of something. And Elizabeth was shaking her head, as if she were refusing to cooperate.

Mark wished he knew what they were talking about.

As soon as Todd and Elizabeth rounded the corner of the nearby administration building, a woman stepped out from behind a tall hedge and hurried after them.

Hmmmm. Interesting. She appeared to be following them.

But why?

The woman didn't look like a Santos flunky. And she was too old to be a student. But something about her was too flamboyant for her to be part of the faculty.

So who was she?

Chapter Four

Louis crossed the campus at a dead run. His heart pounded inside his chest like a hammer and his lungs felt as if they were about to burst.

He had driven from his beach condo to the campus like a madman. He'd run two red lights and a stop sign, practically broadsided a city bus, and barely missed a group of students crossing the wide boulevard that separated the school from the surrounding neighborhood.

When he reached the SVU campus, there had been no open spaces in the faculty parking lot, so he had simply driven up onto the grass and stopped the car. He left it there with the keys in the ignition and the door open.

Louis glanced at his watch. Exactly forty-five minutes ago the phone had rung and started one of the longest nightmares of his life. He had reached for it, half hoping, half fearing that the caller was Jessica.

"Hello," he said breathlessly.

There was no answer.

"Hello?" he repeated.

Through the phone, he heard the distant sound of tires screeching and a horn honking.

"Hello?" he said again.

"Who is she?"

Louis's heart sank. "Leave her alone," he said evenly.

There was a laugh on the other end of the line. A laugh punctuated with static.

"Where are you?" he asked.

"I'm in a car," she said calmly. *"Going about eighty miles an hour. Guess who's in front of me? About five inches in front of me."*

Louis heard another squeal of tires, and he felt the fear in his heart radiate through his body. "What are you doing?" he whispered.

"I'm getting ready to run Blondie off I-87 at the Pine Bluff construction site," she replied calmly. *"I'm going to kill her, Louis. And I just thought you might like to listen while I do it."*

For almost fifteen minutes Louis had listened to the sickening sounds of cars honking, tires squealing, metal tearing, and concrete crashing. Over and over he had begged and pleaded for Jessica's life.

But to no avail. When the phone call had abruptly terminated with a horrible screeching sound, he'd hung up the phone and driven straight to campus.

He had no idea what the outcome of the chase had been. He didn't even know if Jessica was alive. His lungs felt as if they were about to collapse as he ran up the front steps of Dickenson Hall, and his heart raced like a ticking bomb. The blood drummed in his ears so loudly, he could hardly hear his own voice when he called out her name.

"Jessica!" he shouted, jerking open the front doors of Dickenson Hall. Three female students dressed in running clothes stood chatting in the lobby. At the sound of his voice they gave him a curious, almost frightened look. "Jessica Wakefield," he panted. "Where does Jessica Wakefield live? What room?" His tie was unknotted, his shirttail was out, and his tweed jacket had slipped halfway off his shoulders.

They backed slightly away, as if he were insane. He lurched forward. "Tell me what room!" he thundered. "Now!"

"Twenty-eight," one of them answered breathlessly.

He heard them whisper and burst into giggles behind him when he ran for the fire door. His loafers made a clanging noise on the metal stairs. On the second floor he slammed into the door with his shoulder and pushed it open. He moved his head back and forth, looking at the numbers on the doors and trying to get his bearings. He let the door close behind him with a tremendous, reverberating slam, then raced down the hall until he reached room twenty-eight.

Without knocking, Louis threw open the door. "Jessica!" he cried. In an instant he saw her lying facedown on her bed. From the way her shoulders were shaking, he could tell that she was crying. But when she heard his voice, she sat up.

Before she could say a word, he had crossed the room and gathered her in his arms. He buried his face in her neck. "Thank God. Thank God. Thank God," he chanted in a faint whisper.

"Louis," he heard her choke. "You shouldn't be here. You . . ."

She was talking, but he couldn't listen. He couldn't do anything but hold her. The relief was so overwhelming, his legs began to shake. He sank to the floor, pulling her with him. He cradled her in his arms and smothered her face and hair with kisses. With every touch, he tried to reassure himself that she was alive and well. "I love you," he finally managed to say in a coherent voice. "And I thought you were . . ." He broke off, unable to finish the sentence.

Somehow she extricated herself from his arms. "I thought you were single," she said in a cold voice.

Her words were like a bucket of icy water. Relief gave way to shame and sadness.

Her lips were trembling and her eyes were red and swollen. "I ran into your wife." She laughed bitterly and stood. "I guess I should say she ran into me. As a matter of fact, she tried to kill me."

"I know," Louis said quietly, standing himself.

"She called me from her car. I heard the chase. I heard the crashing and the tires and . . ." The fear came rushing back and he reached for Jessica again. But she drew away. "Don't look at me like that," he pleaded.

"You're married," she said simply. Then her face crumpled and her shoulders shook. "Why didn't you tell me?" she sobbed.

His hands hovered helplessly over her shoulders. If he touched her, she would recoil. But he had so much to communicate, words alone weren't enough. "Will you listen to me, please? I need to explain what my wife is."

"Inconvenient?" Jessica asked sarcastically, turning her back to him.

"That person is legally my wife, but she's not the woman I married."

He took off his jacket and tugged at his tie. Even loose, it was choking him. "Her name is Chloe. I met her in North Dakota when I was in graduate school. She was working at a local bookstore. She had no family. And no friends in the area. She said she had grown up out of the country. To make a long story short, we married. Within a few months, she got the idea in her head that I was having an affair with another student. A classmate." Louis pushed back his hair and sat down on the edge of Jessica's bed. "I wasn't. Carol was just a friend from the history department. But Chloe told her—in no uncertain terms—to stay away from me. Carol told her there

37

was nothing going on between us and . . ." Louis swallowed, fighting the nausea that threatened to overwhelm him. "Jessica, to this day I don't know exactly what happened. But Carol left school abruptly. She disappeared and left no forwarding address."

Jessica turned, her face curious. "You think Chloe did something to her?"

"I didn't at the time. I just thought maybe there had been some family emergency. But now, I'm sure she did. Because Carol was just the first. It happened again, with another friend. Chloe became more obsessive. More and more paranoid. People began to file complaints with the police. The situation got so sticky that we left town the day I graduated. I knew there was no way I could get a job in that area after all the things that she had done—slashing tires, breaking people's windows, making threatening calls. I'd tried to get help for her, but . . ." He shook his head. All attempts to help Chloe had been useless.

Jessica turned to face him. Her face was still hard, but he had her attention. And she was listening. "Go on," she said.

"We moved to Seattle. I got a teaching job. For a couple of months everything was fine. Then the pattern started over." He sighed and stretched the muscles in his neck, which felt like tight elastic bands. "She was jealous of everybody who ever spoke to me. She was jealous of my *dog*. I found

38

him dead in the backyard one day." He took some deep breaths to calm himself.

"I told her it was over and I left. I moved to Oregon. I got a job teaching in a little school there. After a while, I began meeting a couple of friends on a regular basis for dinner. One of them was a woman—Marie."

"Marie had an accident while she was cleaning the gutters of her house. The ladder collapsed underneath her, and she fell and broke her neck. She died instantly, and I was devastated. I thought it was just one of those strange and tragic accidents."

Jessica's eyes widened and he swallowed, wondering if he sounded as paranoid and delusional as Chloe. "At the funeral," he said slowly, "I kept smelling her perfume. Chloe's perfume. It's very distinctive. It smells like . . ."

"Roses?" Jessica said, her nose wrinkled in distaste as she remembered the odor.

Louis nodded. "Yes. Roses. I thought it was my imagination. And then when I got home, she was sitting in my living room. She said she had been in therapy. She wanted to try to put our marriage back together. I agreed. After all, she was my wife. And I still hadn't connected Marie's death with her appearance. But a week later, my other friend was killed by a hit-and-run driver. Then I was convinced that Chloe was behind their deaths."

Jessica's eyes were large and unblinking. "Did you tell the police?"

He nodded again. "They didn't find any hard evidence connecting Chloe with either death. And when they found out *I* had left *her*, they decided I was just a philandering husband looking for a cheap and convenient way to get rid of his suspicious wife. They told me if I wanted a divorce, I had to file for one like everybody else."

Jessica flopped back on her bed with a sigh. Apparently Louis still hadn't gotten that divorce.

He took a deep breath and continued. "When I got home, she was gone. Her clothes. Her papers. Everything. She had disappeared without a trace. So that I *couldn't* file for a divorce, you see?"

He stood up and began to pace. Telling the whole story felt good. He'd never revealed to anyone all the sordid details. "I moved again. I got another job. And this time I hired a private detective to do some investigating. As it turned out, Chloe had a history of mental illness and violent behavior going back to her childhood. Her entire family died in a fire when she was twelve. The police report said the cause appeared to be arson. No suspect was ever found."

"You think . . ." Jessica's voice was trembling. Her large blue-green eyes reflected the horror of what Louis had just implied.

He shut his eyes for a moment. "I think she set the fire. I believe she killed her family. And I'm positive she killed my friends."

Louis was so deep into his story that time

seemed to be standing still. He remembered the immense sadness that had overwhelmed him when he'd become convinced that his wife was a woman with no conscience, no sense of right or wrong. The pain was as fresh today as it had been during those long months of piecing together the extent of Chloe's insanity.

"After I found out about the fire, I packed up again and left. My own dad had died and left me some money, so I spent two years just moving around. I finally realized that *I* was in no danger from her. But any friend, any lover, any contact *was*. So I haven't had any. For years. No real friends. No contacts. No lovers. Until you."

Jessica stood up from the bed and stepped toward him. He wrapped his arms around her shoulders and rested his cheek on top of her head. "When I told you we couldn't be together, it wasn't because of the job. It wasn't because I didn't love you. The truth is that staying away is the only way I know of to protect you."

"What now?" she asked softly.

"I leave. I leave SVU. I leave you." Louis ran a hand through his soft hair. "And she'll follow me and let you alone. You'll be safe once I'm gone."

"No!" She threw herself at his chest and her arms clenched him around the waist. "Louis," she pleaded. "You can't go. I don't care what happens to me. I don't want you to leave me. I've never loved anybody like this before, and if you go I'll . . ."

Her passion was infectious and his body

41

throbbed with echoing desire. His own youth had been spent running from an insanely jealous wife. Year after year, he had more completely isolated himself from friends and companionship. The soft touch of another's hand was an almost forgotten sensation until Jessica had come into his life.

He had never been in love with a woman the way he was in love with Jessica. But he had only one option. He had to leave her—as quickly as possible.

The door opened and both Jessica and Louis whirled around, startled.

Louis blinked and shook his head. Was he losing his mind? A girl who looked exactly like Jessica was standing in the doorway. But unlike Jessica, she was glaring at him.

Lila took a sea-green dress off a rack in the Like Wow Boutique, one of her favorite stores. She turned to the mirror and held the dress up under her chin to see what the color did for her. Not much. Lila's eyes were blue and her hair was brown with gold highlights. This shade of green washed her out completely.

She put the dress back on the rack without too much regret. The last hour had been well spent in the sportswear department. She'd found four new outfits and her frazzled nerves were feeling better already.

Ever since childhood, shopping had been therapeutic for Lila. Whenever something bad happened, her father had taken her to the toy store and let her pick out anything she wanted. When she got a little older, he took her to music stores and clothing boutiques.

As a result, shopping was Lila's coping mechanism. Her philosophy was simple: When in doubt, shop. When in despair, shop. When in love, shop. When in confusion, shop.

Luckily she had always had plenty of money to spend. Her father was one of the richest men in California, and she had been raised like a princess. Now Lila flipped idly through the rack while she waited for the salesgirl to ring up her purchases from the sportswear department.

When she had walked into this shop an hour ago, she had been practically in tears. Now she felt ready to go back to her apartment. *Our apartment,* she mentally amended.

This living-together stuff was harder than she had expected. When she and her boyfriend, Bruce Patman, had moved in together, she had pictured them in some really luxurious setting. Every night would be like a scene from a romantic movie. She had visualized candles, music, and silk kimonos that coordinated with the drapes.

Ha! Living with Bruce wasn't turning out as she'd expected. They weren't redecorating a beachfront condo, the way they'd planned. They were living in a dump. Because it was cheap.

She couldn't quite believe it was true. She, Lila Fowler, was living in a crummy attic apartment with no hot water, a dirty kitchen, and a tiny bathroom.

But she was doing it for love. If she and Bruce wanted to be together right now, living like paupers was the only choice they had. Between them, they could hardly come up with enough cash for the deposit.

Bruce's trustee was opposed to the scheme—and so was Lila's dad. The result was that the trustee, Bruce's eccentric uncle Dan, had decided to cut off Bruce's income.

Technically Lila was a woman of independent means. Aside from her own family money, she'd inherited a large estate from her late husband, Count Tisiano di Mondicci. Unfortunately, right now the money was tied up in Italy. She might have to wait months to gain access to what was rightfully hers.

Lila's fingers brushed a silk scarf, instinctively looking for something soft and comforting. Thinking about Tisiano still hurt. She had met him the summer after she graduated from high school. When they had impulsively married, Lila had thought that her life was going to continue like a fairy tale.

But tragedy had struck almost immediately—Tisiano had been killed in a Jet Ski accident. Shortly after his funeral, Lila had returned to Sweet Valley and tried to pick up her life where she had left off.

But it was hard. Her life was different from

everybody else's in some way that was hard to define. Jessica understood to some extent, since she'd been married as well. But Jessica's marriage to Mike McAllery had been short and unhappy, while Lila's marriage to Tisiano had been short and blissful. She lifted the scarf and put her cheek against it. *Don't think about him,* she scolded herself.

She dropped the scarf and lifted her chin, composing herself. Tisiano was her past. Bruce was her present. And her future. She'd just have to accept that until her father's lawyers could untangle her financial affairs, the only money she had was the allowance her father gave her and her credit card.

She had gone through her allowance. Thank goodness for the credit card.

"Excuse me." The salesgirl had appeared and she was holding out Lila's card. "I'm sorry. But your card has been turned down."

"What?" Lila asked, her mouth falling open.

"They said you're over your limit." The salesgirl shrugged apologetically. "Would you rather pay by check?"

Lila dropped her face into her hands. She couldn't write a check. She had zero cash in the bank. And she couldn't ask her dad for more because he wasn't supposed to know she and Bruce were living together.

For the first time in life, Lila Fowler was flat broke.

Chapter
Five

Jessica watched Louis and her sister stare at each other. Louis looked bewildered, and Elizabeth's eyes were narrowed with suspicion.

Louis had just explained his marital situation to Elizabeth. And Elizabeth had explained to Louis what she suspected about the athletics department.

Jessica's head was reeling. Insane wives. Gamblers. Corruption. The puzzle had a million pieces. But the most important piece of it all was Louis. He loved her. She knew he loved her. And knowing that fact made everything else bearable.

Louis ran his hands through his wavy brown hair, pushing it back to reveal the widow's peak that gave his masculine face its sensitive quality. "Obviously, exposing this kind of corruption is more important than my teaching job." He sat on the edge of Jessica's bed and put his arm around her waist. "But I'm worried about Jessica. If you keep investigating and go to the police, it's not just a matter of bad publicity, it's dangerous. For both of you. I can't go off and leave her, or you either, for that matter, in the middle of this. But if I stay, Chloe stays too. And she's just as dangerous as T. Clay Santos."

Elizabeth's gaze fell on his arm and her eyelids lowered halfway in what Jessica recognized as her twin's disapproving look.

"Why did you two have to be seen together?" Elizabeth muttered resentfully.

She went over to the window and gazed outside, her back rigid. Jessica squeezed Louis's hand and slipped out of his embrace. She went and stood at Elizabeth's shoulder. "Liz. I know you have very definite ideas about what's right and what's wrong."

"You're right," Elizabeth replied in a low tone. "I do."

"Then you have to do what you think is right."

"For once, I don't know what's right," Elizabeth said angrily.

"I do." Jessica smiled wistfully and pulled affectionately at her twin's ponytail. "For the first and maybe the only time in my life, I know what's right for all of us. You need to expose this corruption. These people are ruining careers and lives—you have to stop them. You can't worry about me."

"That's impossible," Elizabeth said thickly.

Tears of frustration rolled down her cheeks. "You're my identical twin. I can't *not* worry about you."

Jessica let go of Elizabeth's ponytail and put her arms around her. "I'm grown up now." She kissed Elizabeth on the cheek and walked briskly to her closet, pulling a duffel bag off the top shelf.

"What are you doing?" Louis asked.

"I'm getting ready to leave with you," Jessica said in a firm voice she hardly recognized as her own.

Louis and Elizabeth were suddenly both talking at once. Objecting. Arguing. Refusing.

"Quiet!" she ordered after a few moments. "Both of you be quiet and listen to me."

Louis and her sister obediently fell silent while Jessica opened her bureau drawer and began rifling through the contents. "I'm going." Jessica pulled a heavy black sweater and two T-shirts from her drawer and dropped them into the duffel bag. She opened the next drawer and threw a handful of underwear and bras into the bag. A pair of jeans and a pair of khakis were folded on the top shelf of her closet and she pulled them down, rolled them up, and placed them in the bag. "Louis and I will leave. Together."

"If he takes you with him, his career will be effectively over," Elizabeth argued.

"My career is over already," Louis said. "But I still can't take you with me."

"Why not?" Jessica demanded. She grabbed a

48

bottle of shampoo and her makeup bag off the top of the dresser and threw them into the bag. "Louis, there's no choice anymore. We've got to disappear. Once we're out of the way, Liz can do what she needs to do. And we've got to move fast and get as far away from Chloe as we can." She bent down, fished a pair of sneakers from the bottom of the closet, and dropped them in the bag. She closed the duffel with a loud and decisive zip.

Louis's face was white, and his eyes clearly reflected his indecision. Jessica stood on her toes and brushed her lips against his. Her mind felt sharper and more focused than it had in a long time. "If I don't go, I'm in Elizabeth's way. I'm just one more person she has to worry about. And I could be in danger. So I might as well go with you—at least until all of this blows over. Then we can rethink things."

Louis hesitated and glanced at Elizabeth, as if asking for her blessing. Her sister's face remained stony, and Jessica understood why. Louis's wife might be crazy, but he was still a married man. And he was also a teacher. They were about to embark on a course of action that had the potential to ruin both of their futures. Elizabeth would never give her blessing to such a venture.

As Jessica's eyes pleaded with Elizabeth, she saw her twin's face relent, just as it had relented a million times in the course of their lives. "Go," Elizabeth said finally. A tear rolled down her cheek and her lips formed a trembling smile. She grabbed

49

Jessica's blue jean jacket from the chair and held it out. "Hurry. Every minute counts now."

Jessica put her arms around Elizabeth and held on as tightly as she could. It was impossible to know when they would see each other again. "I know you don't approve," she said into Elizabeth's ear. "And I know you don't believe me. But I do love him. This time it's the real thing. And nothing else matters."

"I know," Elizabeth whispered back, laughing through her tears. "I do believe you. Because this is the only time I've ever seen you leave to go anywhere with less than five pieces of luggage."

Jessica laughed and drew back her head. "Be careful," she told her sister. With that, she kissed her on the cheek and then stepped back, taking her place beside Louis.

"You be careful too," Elizabeth choked.

The two girls flew into each other's arms again for one last embrace.

Louis stepped out of the room to give the sisters a few moments alone. He wouldn't go back to the condo. The place was too dangerous. Based on what Elizabeth had said, somebody was watching his home.

He hovered in the hallway, torn. He felt a certain amount of responsibility for both girls. Should he insist that Elizabeth call in the police? Should he call them himself?

No. He had been that route before. If he did that, he'd have to suffer through interminable interviews and questioning. *Professor Miles, we'd like to ask that you remain in the area until this matter has been thoroughly investigated.*

Every delay put Jessica's life in danger.

Elizabeth seemed like a very competent young woman. And from her description, he surmised that Todd Wilkins was an able partner. Louis just had to hope that she had enough sense to hand this thing off to the authorities if the situation got too dangerous.

His first priority was Jessica. He was responsible for getting her into this mess. And it was his responsibility to keep her safe. Moving targets were the hardest to hit. So they had to get moving. And keep moving.

Elizabeth walked out the back door of Dickenson Hall and into the parking lot with the keys to the Jeep in her hand. For now, she and Jessica had agreed to hold off on calling the insurance company.

If they called the insurance company, the authorities there would contact their parents. And if Mr. and Mrs. Wakefield got wind of anything that was going on, they'd pull Elizabeth out of school and have the police looking for Jessica.

Elizabeth couldn't risk answering any of the questions that would inevitably arise from the incident. But she did want to take a look at the Jeep

51

and see how bad the damage was. She just hoped it was still drivable.

Elizabeth let out an involuntary whistle when she saw it. The Jeep looked like something that had been in a demolition derby. She leaned down and squinted. What was that thing hanging out of the back? The muffler?

Suddenly she screamed. Something was pulled down over her head. A bag or a large piece of canvas. Her arms flailed, but whoever was attacking her was taller and stronger than she was. The assailant yanked her savagely off balance, thrusting her to the side.

Elizabeth's muscles flinched. She threw out her hands to break her fall, expecting to hit concrete. But instead, she fell against something upholstered. Rough hands shoved her farther into what was obviously a car. For a stunned moment Elizabeth was too surprised to react, and her attacker grabbed her hands and tied them behind her back. "Let me go!" she yelled. But the door slammed shut.

Seconds later the driver's-side door banged and the car was in motion. "Shut up, Blondie," the driver growled.

Bruce Patman handed the saleslady his credit card. He and Lila had started the day badly, but he hoped a dozen roses, a bottle of her favorite mineral water, and a gourmet dinner would soothe her ruffled feathers.

Actually, the problems had started last night—when she had practically blown him up with the gas oven. Not knowing how the appliance worked, she'd turned on the jets and neglected to light the pilot. He'd accused her of ignorance, she'd accused him of being a pig, and out of nowhere a huge argument had erupted.

Nope, their first night in their apartment had not exactly been a success. He'd acted like a jerk, and now he needed to make amends to the woman he loved.

Dinners 'n' Things was the ultimate yuppie takeout service. They provided everything one could possibly need for a romantic dinner for two. Flowers. Food. They even had scented candles. Bruce looked around the store and sniffed appreciatively. The air was heavy with the spicy and pungent smell of expensive delicacies. The food from this place was great, and the whole atmosphere had an upscale, European flair.

He scratched the stubble on his cheek. Since Lila had spent the whole morning in the bathroom, he hadn't been able to get in to shave. Of course, the hint of a beard *was* kind of sexy. Unfortunately, it made his face itch. And there was nothing sexy about a man who scratched.

Remembering that the apartment had no hot water, Bruce decided he'd stop at Sigma house on the way home to shower and shave. Then, when he appeared at the door with an armful of flowers and a basket of gourmet food, he would be looking his handsome best.

Lila would fall into his arms, and at last they could have the kind of romantic night he'd been dreaming about since they decided to move in together. He closed his eyes, picturing Lila's slinky figure prowling around the apartment in something filmy and ultra-feminine.

"Excuse me, sir?"

Bruce opened his eyes. The saleslady dangled his credit card from her fingertips as if it were a dirty sock. "The card's been declined," she informed him.

"Declined? What does that mean?" Bruce stared at the woman, unable to grasp the implication of her statement.

She lowered her head and gazed at him over the tops of her glasses. "It could mean any number of things," she said in a damp tone. "Perhaps the card has been stolen."

"I did not steal this card," Bruce retorted. He whipped his wallet out of his back pocket, whisked his driver's license from its plastic sheath, and held it up for her to inspect. "See. Bruce Patman. Same as the name on the credit card."

"Maybe the card has been abused."

"Abused? What do you mean, abused?"

"Perhaps your account is delinquent," she said, maintaining her annoyingly impersonal tone.

Bruce cast his mind over his check register. Nope. He'd paid last month's bill—in full—which was one reason he had no cash this month. "Listen, lady," he began in an antagonistic voice. Then he broke off, hearing his eighty-five-year-old uncle Dan's querulous voice echoing in his memory.

Uncle Dan was Bruce's trustee, which meant he held Bruce's purse strings. The minute he had gotten wind that Bruce had moved in with Lila, he had snapped the purse shut, cutting off Bruce's money. Uncle Dan had insisted that his job was to see that Bruce didn't throw his money away. He didn't approve of his nephew spending money on an apartment when his room and board at Sigma House were paid up through the end of the semester.

Furthermore, Uncle Dan was a bachelor with a deep distrust of the opposite sex. Even though Bruce had explained to him that the Fowler family was one of the richest in the country, Uncle Dan remained convinced that Lila was a fortune hunter dedicated to spending Bruce's money.

The saleslady stared at him, patiently waiting for him to deliver the rest of his tirade. Bruce swallowed his words with a humiliated gulp.

His credit cards were drawn on the brokerage house that managed his trust portfolio. Apparently Uncle Dan had not only cut off his cash, he had canceled his credit card.

Elizabeth tumbled onto the floor of the backseat when the car came skidding to a stop. She didn't know whether to be grateful that the driver had finally reached a destination or even more frightened than she already was.

The ride had been short but terrifying. The SVU campus was surrounded by a town, but ten minutes in any direction led to the California wilderness. If a person wanted to dispose of a body and have the corpse stay hidden for a long time, they wouldn't have to drive too far out of town to find a perfect spot.

The driver's door opened and shut with a slam. Then the back door opened and somebody grabbed Elizabeth by the shoulder and pulled her from the back of the car with her hands still tied behind her back.

"This way," a voice ordered.

Stumbling, Elizabeth struggled to walk with her abductor over a rocky patch of ground.

The bag was snatched suddenly off her head, and the burst of sunlight blinded her. Elizabeth turned her head, squinting, and let the air cool her hot face. Gradually the sunspots cleared. But as soon as she viewed her surroundings, she almost wished for the dark again.

She was standing on the edge of a cliff. In front of her there was a sheer, fifty-foot drop. Her heart began to pound. "Look, whoever you are. You can tell Mr. Santos that it won't do any good to kill me. Too many people know what's going on."

"What are you talking about?"

Elizabeth turned her head and sucked in her breath with a surprised gasp. "Who are you?"

An extremely beautiful woman with masses of

dark, curling hair towered over her. Elizabeth was tall, but this woman must have been six feet. There was something larger than life about her. Her figure was full. Her mouth was large and painted a vivid red—so red it was almost black. Her dark, troubled eyes were enormous. And she was staring at Elizabeth with obvious confusion. Moments later, her eyes reflected dawning wonder. "You're not the same girl," she breathed.

Elizabeth's legs began to tremble. So this was Louis's wife. No wonder he had been so terrified on Jessica's behalf. There was something horrifying and repellent about her beauty.

"You look like her, but . . ." The woman's voice trailed off.

"I think you mixed me up with my sister," Elizabeth managed to say, trying hard to sound reasonable. She took a deep breath and pretended she wasn't standing on the lip of a fifty-foot bluff with a homicidal maniac. "People get us confused a lot."

"Where is your sister?"

Elizabeth smiled and tried to laugh. "Gosh. I really don't know. Can you give me some idea what this is about? Maybe I could help you."

Chloe grabbed her shoulder and shoved her off balance, sending her tumbling forward. Elizabeth screamed. Chloe grabbed her sweater and pulled her back just enough so that she now dangled precariously over the edge. "Tell her to leave Louis alone."

Elizabeth was so frightened, she could hardly answer. Her breath was coming in shallow gulps, and the muscles in her legs and stomach quivered.

Chloe let out a little slack and Elizabeth fell slightly forward. Her breath became so shallow that she felt as if her lungs would never again take in enough oxygen to keep her alive.

"Tell her not to bother denying what's going on. I saw her leaving his condo this morning. I took some pictures with a telescopic lens. I slid them under the door of the administrative office. He's probably getting fired right now." She laughed. "Poor Miles. When will he learn that without me, his life isn't worth living? Tell her to leave him alone or she'll be sorry. And so will you."

Chapter Six

"Wow!" Denise said. "I can really feel that work-out in the muscles of my calves."

"Uh-huh," Winston answered dully. He lifted his fork wearily to his lips. It was dinnertime, and they were sitting before large plates of food. They had both showered and put on clean uniforms before coming to the cafeteria.

"What a day!" Denise continued, hoping to spark a little life into Winston. "ROTC is like a marathon workout." She smiled brightly. "But it's invigorating. Right? I mean, don't you feel more fit than you've ever felt in your life?"

Winston grunted and fished around in his noodles for a piece of chicken.

Denise put down her fork and tugged at her cuffs. "I like this uniform. It feels crisp." She gazed down at the sharply pressed creases of her sleeves. The dignified suit was a nice change from the floppy rayons and wilted silks she usually salvaged from local thrift shores.

Denise had always been a funky fashion devotee. She and Winston both. They loved putting together wild outfits. And they often swapped shirts. Sometimes Denise even wore Winston's pants—rolled up at the ankle. But she giggled at the idea of Winston in her pants.

Denise was petite, with an almost perfect figure. Winston was tall and skinny with perpetually messy hair that framed his handsome face. Through a series of mishaps, he had wound up as the only male resident of Oakley Hall, an all-female dorm. He and Denise had started out as dorm friends, and from there the relationship had grown into love.

Winston still said nothing. As she watched him lift another forkful of noodles, Denise felt a slight flicker of annoyance. Winston was one of those men who had a perennially rumpled appearance. Even in freshly starched and pressed military garb, he managed to look wrinkled and loosely hinged.

"Winston," she said, an edge of impatience in her voice. "Can't you sit up a little straighter? You're so bent over you look like a question mark."

Winston's fork hovered in front of his mouth, and he stared across the table with a hurt expression that immediately brought out her protective instincts. "I didn't mean to sound critical," she said in a softer tone. "It's just that, well, when you sit like that you look sort of . . . weak."

"Weak?"

"I don't mean weak weak. I mean . . ." She trailed off when she saw a dangerous glint in his eye.

Winston put down his fork and this time, he did sit up straight. "Denise. I appreciate your joining ROTC so we could be together. It was, well . . . an incredible gesture. But if you're going to make that Drake clown your role model . . ."

"You mean *Lieutenant Drake*?" Her voice held a little note of warning. She could feel her protective instincts fading fast. Winston's mouth fell open in surprise at her tone. "You've got a crush on that guy, don't you?" he accused.

She blushed and stabbed her meatball with a fork. "Of course not."

"Then why are you sticking up for him like that? And why are you picking on me? *Winston*," he mimicked. "*Sit up straighter. You look like you're having a weak attack.* You sound like my mother."

"Shhhhh," she warned, darting a nervous look around the cafeteria. She would be really embarrassed if anybody overheard this conversation. "I do *not* have a crush on Lieutenant Drake," she insisted. "But I do admire him."

Winston rolled his eyes. "I can't believe this. The guy's a sadistic boot camp officer—right out of some slapstick comedy about the military."

"He is not," Denise argued. "Sure, he gets a little carried away. But that's because he's going to make a career out of the military. He's an officer. He has faith in his ability to lead. You could learn some valuable lessons from him if you'd let yourself."

"Denise! Come *on*. The guy's a joke. The whole thing is a joke."

Suddenly Winston's whole personality, persona, and—most of all—his posture seemed incredibly irritating. "Winston," she said, narrowing her eyes. "You're going to have to shape up. We're talking commitment time now. You're always telling me how much you care about me. You're always talking about how committed you are. But so far, I haven't ever seen you commit to anything more important than a practical joke. If you want to prove to me that you can be serious about a relationship, then you need to be serious about the promise you made to the Reserve Officers' Training Corps. Do I make myself clear?"

Winston opened his mouth to make a smart remark. In response she lifted her chin, warning him not to say something he'd regret. For once she wasn't going to be cajoled out of her mood. He backed down and said nothing, contenting himself with giving her an ironic salute across the table.

Denise didn't respond. She lowered her eyes to her plate and stared at her green peas. She'd lost her appetite. Had Winston Egbert always been such a child? Had he always been this immature and whiny?

She pictured Lieutenant Drake. She had seen him smile and joke with some of the members of the unit. He had a sense of humor. But he acted like a real man. And she couldn't deny that she found his undeniable masculinity a very attractive quality.

Todd lay on his bed, wearing the track shorts and old, soft T-shirt he used for pajamas. He couldn't sleep, and his mind kept going over the events of the day while he stared at the ceiling. He hadn't seen Elizabeth since they left the athletics complex. She had promised to talk to Jessica again and feel her out on what might happen if they pursued their investigation. She'd said she'd call him when she reached a decision, but so far he hadn't heard a word from her.

Since he knew the investigation was weighing heavily on Elizabeth's mind, he was sure she'd contact him as soon as she had something concrete to say. The twins were probably still hashing things out.

A soft knock at his door startled him. Todd rolled out of bed, tense and alert. He didn't have a roommate, and since returning to school after his suspension, he hadn't had a chance to make many friends.

Nobody ever "dropped in." Could it be Bobbo or some other thug on Santos's payroll? "Who is it?" he asked cautiously.

"It's me, Liz. Let me in."

Todd unlocked the door, and Elizabeth practically fell inside the room. Her clothes were a mess, and her hair was all over the place. There was a long scratch on her cheek. "Elizabeth! What happened to you?" He caught her shoulders as she stumbled, steadying her.

"I met Mrs. Louis Miles," she said in an exhausted voice.

"Huh?"

Todd's room had its own bathroom, which Elizabeth staggered into. She turned on the faucet in the sink, splashing cold water onto her face. Todd came in behind her and handed her a towel. Then he began rummaging through the medicine cabinet for some cotton pads and hydrogen peroxide.

Elizabeth reached for his brush, which lay on the counter, and tugged it through her tangled hair. She managed to remove most of the leaves and stickers, but she still looked as if she'd just returned from a wilderness survival course. When Todd reached over and dabbed at the scratch with hydrogen peroxide, she winced.

"Professor Miles has a wife," Elizabeth explained through clenched teeth. "She's completely insane. And dangerous. She came close to throwing me off a cliff but changed her mind when she realized I wasn't Jessica." She took the cotton ball from his hand and finished patting the scratch. "It's just a flesh wound," she said, doing her John Wayne imitation.

"You sure seem calm about all this," Todd said, following her back into his room.

She sank into his desk chair and let out a long groan. "When you walk what feels like ten miles in the dark, you have a lot of time to think things through and get them in perspective. I'm alive. And Jessica is safe for now. Louis, too. Jessica threw some things in a bag and they left so we could keep on with what we're doing. The investigation is back on."

"Where did they go?" Todd asked, perching on the side of his bed.

Elizabeth stretched her arms, looking troubled. "I don't know. We'll talk about it some more tomorrow. But I think I'd better sleep here tonight. If Chloe went back to Professor Miles's condo, it won't take her long to figure out that he and Jessica have split. It might make her mad enough to change her mind and try to throw me off that cliff again." Elizabeth massaged her temples. "If she comes looking for me in my room, I don't want to be there. Wake me up early, will you?"

Elizabeth moved to Todd's extra twin bed and flopped down, not bothering to get under the covers. Todd scratched his jaw and watched Elizabeth roll over and close her eyes. He'd never seen her look so tired. She didn't stir when he leaned over and pulled off her boots and socks. She was asleep.

He looked down at her now peaceful face. She was an incredibly brave and beautiful woman—he had spent most of his life in love with her. Then he'd come down with an attack of big-man-on-campus-itis and broken up with her shortly after they arrived at college. His idiocy had led to a long estrangement. That was behind them now, and every day they were becoming better and better friends. Every day they were becoming different people, too, getting on with their separate lives.

Elizabeth was in love with Tom Watts now. And Todd was in love with Gin-Yung. Physically, Gin-Yung and Elizabeth had nothing at all in common. Gin-Yung was small, with a boyish disregard for fashion. Her hair was cut in a straight, no-nonsense bob, and she always wore pretty much the same thing—loafers, unpressed khakis, a white cotton shirt, and a blue blazer. He didn't know how she managed to pull off her unique style, but somehow she made the unfashionable ensemble look feminine and endearing.

He missed her. And he knew she'd had her feelings hurt over being excluded from this investigation. But he didn't want to put her in any danger. He'd waited too long to meet someone he could fall in love with to take a chance on losing her now.

Todd turned off the lamp beside his bed, reflecting that he was a very lucky guy to have had two such amazing women in his life. In the dim light that streamed in the window, he took a blanket from his closet and carefully covered Elizabeth. "Good night," he whispered, leaning over and kissing her softly on the cheek. "And thank you for being my friend."

66

Jessica sat beside Louis on a thick hooked rug and gazed into the crackling fire. They were in a cabin in Arizona. Tucked away on a side road, the hideaway was far off the main highway. Louis didn't know whether or not Chloe was on their trail yet, and he didn't want to leave his car in a motel parking lot where it might be spotted by a passerby.

The place they had found turned out to be much nicer than a motel. Each little cabin had its own fireplace and kitchenette. Jessica felt as if they were playing house.

She laid her head in the hollow of Louis's shoulder and rubbed her face against the cloth of his new flannel shirt. She was exhausted from a long, tiring afternoon and night.

They had left the campus, heading east. During the many hours on the road, they'd stopped only twice—once at a truck stop, for gas and food, and once in the main square of a small town. Louis had bought some clothes in a sporting goods store, then stopped at the pharmacy for a toothbrush, comb, and razor.

After that they had driven, mostly in silence, until long after dark. Louis had been tense and quiet, his green eyes flickering constantly back and forth between the road and the rearview mirror. Not until night had fallen and they were hours away from SVU had he begun to unwind a little.

He wrapped his arms around her and pulled

her down until she lay in his lap, staring up at him. There was a deep melancholy in his face, and Jessica lifted her hand, running her finger along his chin. "Louis," she said softly. "Why are you so sad? No matter what happens now, we're together."

He kissed her fingers and opened her hand, laying the palm against his cheek. "I'm sad because I love you, and I know that someday, maybe someday soon, you won't love me. You'll hate me."

She sat up so that she could look directly into his eyes. "Don't say that, because it's not true. I could never hate you."

"I've stolen your life from you," he said. Then his lips moved silently, as if he had no words to describe the enormity of the situation. "This kind of existence is living death. You might as well be dead. Because you're cut off from your family, and from your friends."

Jessica caressed his cheek. "You're my family. You're my friend. You're all I need, Louis. You're all I want."

"I've done a terrible thing, but . . ." He shook his head helplessly. "I don't know what else I could have done."

His face looked so haggard and anguished that Jessica's heart ached for him.

"I've taken your life from you. In return, I've given you nothing."

The love Jessica felt threatened to overwhelm her. She knew now that the only way she would be happy was to see him happy. She decided that she'd try to tease him out of his dark mood. "If it makes you feel any better, I really did enjoy your class, Professor Miles. It wasn't just your good looks that got me to show up. Shall we talk about medieval history?"

Finally he laughed. "I'd rather not talk about the past at all tonight," he said when he caught his breath. He lay back on the rug and leaned his head on his arm. "There's a star," he murmured, looking out the window.

"You should make a wish on the first star of the night."

"A wish?" he asked, gazing at the sky.

"Yes. If you had one wish, what would it be?"

Louis thought for a moment. When he spoke, his voice was almost a whisper. "I would wish for one perfect day with you. A day with no Chloe on our trail. A day with no worries. A day to just be any other couple in love."

Jessica bent her head over his, admiring the glow of his skin in the moonlight. "Sometimes wishes come true," she whispered. "Mine did when I met you."

Lila stared dolefully into the open refrigerator. She didn't know why she was even bothering to look. There hadn't been any food at midnight. So why would there be anything to eat at two A.M.? She was just looking inside out of habit. Most refrigerators had food in them.

But there was nothing in theirs but a lightbulb. She still couldn't believe that Bruce had gone by Sigma House, eaten a huge dinner, and then come home a half an hour ago empty-handed. "I'm starving," she complained. "I wanted you to take me out to dinner."

Bruce was reading a history textbook on the couch. "For the fifteenth time, I'm sorry," he said impatiently. "I tried to call you. Since you weren't in the apartment, I went over to Sigma House to eat. I figured you went out to eat with Jessica or something. So I stuck around and played pool for a while."

Lila slammed the refrigerator door shut. "Why would I go out without telling you?" she asked in a frustrated voice. "We're not roommates, Bruce. We don't just come and go and not tell each other what our plans are. We're *living* together. We're a couple. We sleep together. We eat together. We do things *together*. And if we're not going to do something together, we need to let each other know."

"You expect me to call you for permission to go to Sigma House?" he asked, sitting up straight on the faded couch.

Lila felt her temper rising. Did he really not understand what she was telling him? "Who said anything about permission?" she demanded in a louder voice.

"Shut up!" the tenant below them yelled. The shout was followed by several loud thumps on the ceiling—their floor—with the handle of a broom.

Lila was so irritated that she jumped up and down as hard as she could five times in a row. "*You* shut up," she shouted back.

"Cut it out, Lila. You're going to get us evicted."

"By who?" she demanded. "Our landlady, Mrs. Finch? She got on a bus yesterday, and according to the guy who came to repair the roof, she could be gone for weeks. And if she *were* here, I'd file a complaint against the guy downstairs."

Bruce held out his arms. "I'm sorry, Li. I didn't know you were waiting for me. I didn't know you were hungry. But if it makes you feel any better, I couldn't have taken you out to dinner anyway."

"Why not?"

He sighed. "Uncle Dan canceled my credit card. I guess we'll have to coast on yours for a couple of weeks."

Lila's eyes fluttered shut, and she groaned.

Chapter
Seven

Tom Watts stared at the ceiling of his hotel room in Las Vegas. It was five A.M., but he was still wide awake. Wide awake and worried. He had tried calling Elizabeth up until three, but neither she nor Jessica had answered the phone. Either she was angry and ignoring his calls, or else . . .

Tom turned on his side and closed his eyes tightly. Maybe if he tried hard enough, he could turn off his worries and get a couple hours of sleep. He desperately needed rest. Yesterday had been a full day of seminars. The UBC conference was keeping the student broadcasters very busy.

The new University Broadcasting Company had invited key student broadcast journalists from universities around the country to attend a conference sponsored by the new cable channel. In addition to sitting in on seminars, the students were there to cover the wrestling match between Craig

Maser, from SVU, and Scotty Fisher from the University of Arizona. The match was scheduled to be the premiere broadcast event on the new TV station.

So far, the conference had been a very interesting experience. And if he weren't so worried about Elizabeth, Tom would be having a blast.

Unfortunately, he and Elizabeth weren't on the best of terms right now. When he had left SVU, he had assigned Elizabeth to do a story on alumni donations while he was gone. Since then, she'd called him with some wild theory about financial misdeeds in the athletics department.

He'd told her she was making mountains out of molehills *and* he'd told her she was letting herself be manipulated by Todd Wilkins. Because Elizabeth's investigation of unfair privileges to athletes led to Todd getting kicked off the basketball team, she had always felt responsible for his bad luck. Now Tom figured that Todd was probably guilting Elizabeth into helping him make some kind of trouble for the department.

Tom had ordered Elizabeth to back off from her current story. His order had made her mad. He had called later and tried to apologize, but she hadn't been too receptive. Elizabeth and Todd went back a long way. And Tom couldn't help worrying that Elizabeth's guilt over Todd might be turning into something more like affection. So yesterday, he'd called Gin-Yung.

Gin-Yung was possessive and territorial. He knew

that if there were something going on between Elizabeth and Todd, she'd sense it immediately.

Yesterday she'd said that yes, they were spending a lot of time together. But she was convinced the relationship wasn't romantic. They were working on a story, but she said she couldn't talk about it. Elizabeth and Todd had asked her not to.

Tom had relaxed. Even though he'd told Elizabeth to back off the athletics department, he had a feeling she was ignoring his command and chasing the story around with Wilkins. If they wanted to run after imaginary bad guys and scandals, that was their business.

The worst thing that could happen was that they would waste a lot of time and feel foolish.

Tom flopped over on his other side, pulling the blanket with him. So why couldn't he sleep? And where was Elizabeth? He wondered if he should call Gin-Yung again.

Nahhhh.

Elizabeth wasn't the only one who could make something out of nothing. What Tom needed to do was quit worrying and get some sleep.

"Hurry," Louis urged. He pushed Jessica gently toward the door while carrying both their suitcases. "It's almost light." In the dark of early morning they had gotten up, showered, and dressed hastily.

Jessica made a sudden decision. Then she turned and smiled. "No."

74

"What?"

"I won't hurry. Not today. And neither will you."

An uncertain smile played around his lips. "Jessica, we have to . . ."

"We have to have one perfect day," she said. She reached out and tugged on the bags, forcing him to drop them. She took his arms and arranged them around her waist. "There. That's better." Her arms encircled his neck, and she looked him in the eye. "Today is our perfect day. When the sun comes up, we're going to stop worrying about Chloe. And we're not going to think about her again until the sun goes down."

Louis was smiling and his eyebrows lifted. He looked unsure of his ability to take part in that kind of mental exercise. "I don't . . ."

"Yes, you can," she encouraged. She laughed. "There aren't too many things that I'm really good at—but having fun is one of them. I'm good at ignoring problems, too."

He bit his lower lip.

"And being irresponsible is my best sport. Have you ever done anything irresponsible?"

"Only when I let you stay the night and allowed Chloe to . . ."

She pulled back the curtain of the window and put a finger to his lips. "The sun is coming up. You can't talk about your ex-wife or your old job or my in-the-dumper education or anything else unpleasant. Yesterday you were a teacher. Today

75

you're a student. *My* student. I'm going to teach you how to be irresponsible."

Louis detached the curtain from her fingers and let the cloth fall down over the window, shielding them from view. "Maybe for just one day . . ."

Todd and Elizabeth took the long route to Elizabeth's dorm, keeping to the perimeter of the campus, where there were hedges and walls. "How will I know her if I see her?" he asked, casting his eyes about for signs of Chloe Miles.

"You can't miss her," Elizabeth said, pulling her baseball cap down low over her eyes. "She looks like a psychotic wonder woman."

Elizabeth wore a pair of Todd's jeans, one of his polo shirts, and his baseball cap. Her own clothes had been too dirty and torn to put on this morning. Todd carried them under his arm.

"Hold it. Who's that?" Todd grabbed Elizabeth's arm and pulled her to a stop. Two men were coming out the front door of Dickenson Hall. One of them was Bobbo. They climbed into a generic-looking white truck that seemed identical to the ones parked around campus at the various construction sites. "Looks like you had company," Todd said as he and Elizabeth stepped back into a hedge while the truck passed them.

"Darn," she said. "Boy, am I sorry I missed them."

When the truck disappeared from view, Todd

and Elizabeth darted toward the building. There was no one in the lobby, and they took the stairs to the second floor. When they reached Elizabeth's room, the door was slightly ajar. Slowly and carefully, Todd pushed it open. They both froze. The room was trashed. Totally trashed.

Books were pulled off shelves. Clothes were scattered. The phone was in a million pieces. Elizabeth went over to what was left of the computer and dropped her head into her hands. "Oh no," she breathed. "Everything we had was on that computer. My files. The stats Gin-Yung gave us. The financial records I stole from the athletics office." She pulled open her desk drawer, frantically searching for her box of computer disks. Finding the drawer empty, she groaned. "And they took my backup disks," she said. "We've got nothing."

"Get some clothes together," Todd said, taking her arm and steering her toward the closet. "And let's get out of here."

"Where are we going?"

"I don't know yet, but luckily we have all day to find a place," he said, surveying the damage. "Those guys know where I live too, and I'll bet anything that their next stop is my room. We need to get off the campus."

"My Jeep is totaled," she said.

"My car's in good shape," he said, going over to help her pull her suitcase down from the shelf. "All I need to do is get some gas. If we have to,

77

we can just find a place to park on a side street and sleep in the car tonight."

Jessica turned the collar of her chambray shirt up against the breeze and flexed her booted foot. It was a beautiful New Mexican afternoon. The sky was an almost surreal color of cerulean with puffs of white clouds like wisps of smoke hanging high over their heads.

Louis walked a few feet ahead of her, clearing their path through the beautiful, unspoiled state parkland. There wasn't a soul around for miles, and above her head, she watched a flock of birds soar and disappear behind the golden glare of the sun.

As Louis paused and lifted his head to look at the birds, Jessica's own heart soared. The gray and haggard look Louis had worn yesterday and last night was gone.

He was slipping comfortably into her one perfect day fantasy. So far, everything was perfect. Today they had no past and no undecided future. Today they had each other. And for now, that was enough.

"Here," he said, holding a branch back to reveal a clearing. "This is exactly the kind of place I had in mind."

Jessica stepped into the clearing and gasped at the spectacular view. Then she looked around as if they were newlyweds inspecting an apartment. "Oh, Louis. It's beautiful. But can we *afford* it?"

He laughed, dropping the blanket and the grocery sack. He put his arms around her and pulled her close, bending his head over hers. "Today we can afford anything."

Their kiss was so slow and sensual. There was no hurry, no urgency, and no fear.

"Do teachers enjoy playing hooky as much as students do?" she asked, giggling.

"No," he said. "Teachers become teachers because they like school."

"Louis," she warned.

"I'm not complaining," he said quickly. "And who knows. Maybe I just liked school because I didn't know how much fun hooky was. I didn't have you to teach me, unfortunately." He spread out the blanket they had bought from a roadside stand. There had been vendors all along the highway, and they had bought fruit, bread, vegetables, and cheese. "I'm very happy," he assured her. He dug down into the sack and began fishing out the items. He laughed shortly. "At least I think what I'm feeling is happiness. It's such an odd and unfamiliar sensation, I'm not sure I can accurately identify it."

She knelt down beside him and began unwrapping the hard, flat bread. "The last few years have been hard for you, haven't they? I hate thinking about you being so horribly lonely."

"Then don't think about it," he said. "You're not supposed to think unhappy thoughts today."

His eyes sparkled and his face had an open,

unguarded look that she hadn't seen since that first day when they had spoken in the bookstore. She had thought then that he was a student. He hadn't looked much older than herself.

"Besides," he continued, "if our lives were a book and you had read the book before, think how much pleasure you would get from reading it over again."

She laughed. "Say that again."

He crossed his legs and settled himself more comfortably, handing her an apple and taking one for himself. "Think about it," he said in a cheerful tone. "If we were characters in a book and you knew there was a happy ending for me and for you, the unhappy parts of the book wouldn't make you nearly as sad. Because you would know that everything was going to come out all right in the end. In fact, you would feel that all their suffering and unhappiness was a *good* thing." His face was serious now.

He took a bite of the crisp red apple and chewed thoughtfully. "Because the pain would make them appreciate just how rare and precious a perfect day is. And they would be determined not to waste it." He put down the apple and reached out to touch her.

A cool breeze lifted the tendrils of hair around Jessica's face. She shivered, unsure of whether she was trembling because of his touch, the sudden chill, or the poignancy of his words.

*   *   *

"Egbert! You're slacking," Lieutenant Drake shouted.

"I'm not slacking," Winston argued. "I'm just not good with firearms."

Lieutenant Drake took the rifle from Winston. "Watch me," he ordered curtly. With a seeming flick of the wrist and twist of the elbow, the lieutenant had the gun spinning like a baton. There was a click and a snap. In a flash the gun was parked over Drake's shoulder in a jaunty, military position. "Now you try it again."

Winston gingerly took back the gun. With the entire unit assembled on the drill field, Winston had never felt so self-conscious in his life. Every eye seemed to be on him.

"Present *arms!*" yelled Lieutenant Drake. The command was the signal for all soldiers to launch into the gun-twirling routine that the lieutenant had been demonstrating all afternoon. Everybody else seemed to have learned it, but Winston just kept fumbling. This time, he was determined to succeed.

He took the gun and tried to emulate Lieutenant Drake's quick flick of the wrist. But somehow the small movement went drastically wrong. The next thing Winston knew, the gun had gone flying into the air like a runaway baton.

Lieutenant Drake and the company surrounding him scattered as the gun began its downward ascent. Winston stared upward, and when the rifle came spinning back down—miraculously—he *caught* it.

81

"I got it!" Winston cried happily. He was so excited, he couldn't contain himself. He parked the gun in his arms as if it were a bouquet of flowers and gave the rest of the company a beauty queen wave. "Thank you," he said in a comic voice. "I just want to say that if I'm elected Miss America, I want to work toward world peace, eradicate hunger, and find a cure for split ends." He burst into giggles and waited for the laughs and scattered applause that his antics usually elicited around the dorm.

Nobody laughed. Winston scanned the assembled faces. Nobody looked amused or entertained. In fact, the other members of the ROTC were looking at him as if he were a genuine alien, straight from Mars.

Somebody was laughing, though. Somebody was helplessly convulsed with laughter.

To his horror, Winston realized it was *him*!

For what seemed like hours, he laughed. The silence around him grew deeper and deeper. He was having a hysterical reaction, but he didn't know how to regain his composure. He caught Denise's eye and she looked away, as if she were embarrassed for him.

"Egbert. Control yourself," Lieutenant Drake commanded.

But Winston couldn't control himself. And the sight of Lieutenant Drake glowering just made him laugh harder. *Slap me, somebody. Please, slap me.*

"Egbert!" Lieutenant Drake commanded again. "Stop it."

"I ca . . . ca . . . ca . . ." Even to his own ears, he sounded like a hyena. He was making a complete fool out of himself. He felt as if somebody had flipped the on switch; he wasn't going to be able to stop until somebody pressed off.

Winston saw Denise lower her eyes and stare determinedly at the toes of her boots. She wasn't going to slap him or find his off button. He was on his own.

"Leave the field," Lieutenant Drake said quietly. "Now. And don't come back until you show a little dignity."

Winston staggered away, still laughing, but practically sick to his stomach with humiliation. No matter how much he wanted to deny the truth, Lieutenant Drake had come out of this episode looking like the better man. Not only could he sling a gun around, he could keep a straight face and comport himself with pride when the circumstances required it.

Winston didn't have to be sent from the field like a schoolchild to feel completely crushed. Behind him, he could sense the last bit of Denise's affection for him evaporating into the crisp California air.

Bruce watched Lila pace the floor of their apartment like a caged animal. Neither one of them had any classes today, and Lila hadn't been outside once. Bruce had gone over to Sigma House for lunch and returned with a napkin full of muffins and a cup of coffee for Lila. She had hungrily devoured the food, and now they were trying to figure out how to spend the rest of the afternoon. Bruce still didn't understand why Lila hadn't wanted to go to Theta House for lunch—there was some female pride thing involved.

The apartment was too small and too depressing to hang out in. The tiny rooms looked bad at night, but in the daytime they were positively unacceptable. The only good thing he could say about the apartment was that they didn't have any roaches. The way he saw it, the place was so awful, even bugs didn't want to hang out in it.

Their new home was an attic apartment with one small window. The hardwood floors were covered with scratches, and the carpet-covered areas were badly stained. The curtains were old, dirty, and full of holes. Bruce thought they had once been yellow, but he wasn't sure.

The sofa and chairs were some indeterminate shade of brown that coordinated only with the scorch marks on the lamp shades. The bedroom was tiny and had a slanted ceiling. The kitchen defied description; the bathroom was even worse. They had done the best they could to clean the place up. But they were just two people pitted against twenty-five years' worth of grease and grime.

Bruce was as eager to leave the apartment for the day as Lila, but they couldn't figure out what to do with no money. They couldn't go out to eat or buy any groceries. They couldn't go to the movies. They couldn't shop. He snapped his fingers. "What about taking a walk?" Bruce suggested. "That doesn't cost anything."

"We could do that," Lila said. "But then I'd just work up an appetite, and since we don't have any food, I'd be more unhappy than I am now."

Bruce checked his watch. "They'll be serving dinner at Sigma House in about three hours. If you could hold out until then, I can probably get you a sandwich."

"I can't subsist on what you can forage from Sigma House," she snapped.

Bruce pressed his lips together. He felt totally inadequate. "I guess I'm not excelling in the hunting-and-gathering department," he said quietly. "I'm sorry. This isn't how I imagined living together."

She flew to his side. "I'm sorry too. I guess I'm cranky," she said in a contrite tone that made Bruce feel even worse. Lila was spoiled, but she was really trying hard to make this work. She was making compromises that in a million years he wouldn't have expected her to make.

She might be irritating to be around for long periods, but having seen the sacrifices she'd made, he couldn't call her selfish anymore. In that respect, their attempt at living together was a success. She was changing. Lila was used to the best of everything, and she was suffering all the indignities that went along with poverty and deprivation so that she could be with him. The least Bruce could do was try to come up with some way to meet her basic needs.

"Lila," he said slowly. "I've been giving this a lot of thought. I think there's only one thing to do in a case like this."

"What's that?"

"Go home and raid the refrigerator."

Chapter
Eight

Elizabeth stood at the gas station, leaning against Todd's BMW. He'd just filled his tank with supreme unleaded and had gone inside the station to pay the bill. As she waited anxiously, Elizabeth's mind was racing. They'd been driving around, trying to reconstruct their information. Basically they'd been killing time until they could figure out their next move.

They needed a place to stay. A place where they couldn't be found by either Santos or Chloe, if she was still in the area—which Elizabeth doubted.

A hotel was no good. There weren't very many around town and it would be too easy to find them in one. Just as she was deciding that they needed to hide out in an apartment, she saw Bruce's Porsche pull up next to her.

Bruce jumped out of the car while Lila remained in the front seat, disguised behind a pair of large designer sunglasses. "Elizabeth!" Bruce said with a wide smile. "Man, am I glad to see you."

Elizabeth felt faintly surprised. She and Bruce Patman had known each other since grammar school, but they weren't particularly good friends. Neither were he and Todd.

"Can you lend me some money?" he asked pleasantly.

Elizabeth's eyes widened in astonishment. "*You* want to borrow money from *me*? What happened? Did the stock market crash or something?"

Lila stuck her head out the window. "It's a long story. Could you lend us money for gas, and we'll pay you back when we can?"

Elizabeth reached into the pocket of her jeans and pulled out a few bills. "I'm happy to lend you money," she said with a smile. "On one condition."

Bruce took the money from her fingers and reached for the gas pump. "Anything," he said breezily, untwisting the gas cap.

"Todd and I need a place to stay tonight."

Lila and Bruce both gave her a startled look, and Elizabeth realized that she had given them the wrong impression. But to correct what they were imagining would lead to more questions.

"I didn't know you two were back together," Bruce commented.

"Um. Well. You know . . ." Elizabeth smiled nervously.

Bruce reached into his pocket and handed her

a set of keys on a Sigma key chain. "Fifty-five twenty-one Chester Street. Attic apartment. It's all yours. We'll call you before we come back."

Elizabeth glanced over her shoulder. Todd was emerging from the gas station and lifted his hand to wave at Bruce and Lila. Before he could say anything that would negate the impression that they were madly in love, Elizabeth threw her arms around him.

"Todd!" she breathed. "Bruce and Lila are going to let us use their apartment."

He looked somewhat taken aback by her passionate greeting, but he seemed to catch her big-eyed "play along" signal.

"Gosh, Bruce, Lila. Thanks a lot."

Bruce nodded as Lila peered over her sunglasses at Todd. "It's not very, um . . . romantic," she said in a flat voice.

Todd put his arm around Elizabeth's waist. "I'm sure it's perfect," he said.

Elizabeth smothered a laugh behind her hand.

Two minutes later Bruce and Lila were pulling out of the gas station. Lila rolled up her window and glanced in the sideview mirror at Todd and Elizabeth. "Did you know Todd and Elizabeth were back together?" she asked Bruce.

"I had no idea," he answered absently, checking to make sure no cars were coming before he pulled out into the street. "I wonder if Gin-Yung knows."

"She does now," Lila said.

Bruce looked at Lila. "Huh?"

Lila nodded in the direction of the bookstore across the street. Gin-Yung stood next to the door in her customary khakis, white shirt, blue blazer, and loafers. Her straight black hair was pulled back in a short, sleek ponytail. She stood on the curve, staring intently across the street at Todd and Elizabeth.

"Are you and that Egbert guy . . . um . . . *dating*?" Paula Roberts asked Denise.

Denise hesitated before answering. For the first time since they'd started dating, she found herself *embarrassed* to have Winston for a boyfriend. She felt awful, but she just couldn't help the new sensation. Winston was acting like such an idiot.

Paula was a tall, pretty sophomore with blond hair and brown eyes. She was a new recruit, like Denise. And like Denise, she was excelling. They were engaged in a friendly rivalry, and Denise didn't want to lose face. "Well, we hang around together a lot," she hedged.

The girls were in the middle of a rigorous round of calisthenics. Denise had always had strong abs and a flat stomach. Still, Paula was obviously more athletic, and Denise was proud that she had been able to keep up with her. They had just completed fifty sit-ups and neither girl was winded. Push-ups were next.

"But he's not, like, your *boyfriend*?" Paula pressed.

90

"Oh, no," Denise heard herself saying. "He's not my boyfriend."

"He's not my boyfriend!"
Since when? Winston groaned silently. Unseen by Denise, he had returned to the group and found a place in the row behind her. He'd overheard the two girls talking about him and expected Denise to launch into a big speech about how Winston might not be GI Joe, but he was her man and she was behind him all the way.

But no. She had denied that he was her boyfriend.

Before, he hadn't been able to stop laughing. Now he was afraid he might burst into tears. Just as Winston was swallowing the huge lump in his throat, Denise turned. When she saw his stricken face, the color began to drain from her own cheeks. He could see her mentally replaying the conversation, trying to figure out exactly how much he might have heard.

Winston gave her the most accusing stare he could muster. If she didn't want to admit he was her boyfriend, fine. At the moment he didn't want to admit she was his girlfriend.

No *friend* would have done what she just did.

A sharp whistle pierced the air. "Everybody give me twenty!" Lieutenant Drake shouted. Winston turned his head away, eager to avoid Denise's gaze.

"OK. We've had a picnic, and we've taken a walk. Now what?" Louis said, taking a hand off

91

the steering wheel so that he could squeeze Jessica's fingers.

"We find a town and . . ."

Louis glanced at her, his eyebrows raised. ". . . and . . ."

"And hang out," Jessica said simply.

A sign over the freeway indicated that Santa Fe was only a few miles away. "Does Santa Fe sound like a nice place to *hang out*?" Louis asked pleasantly.

"Santa Fe sounds like a great place to hang out," she responded.

"How, exactly, does one hang out?" Louis asked sardonically.

"Well," Jessica said, leaning her head back on the seat and studying his profile. "The first thing you have to do is take off your watch."

"Hold the wheel," he instructed.

Giggling, Jessica leaned over to steer while he removed his watch. When it was free from his wrist, he dropped the watch in her lap. Then he took the wheel back in his own hands.

Jessica took the watch and put it in the glove compartment next to her makeup bag. A minute later Louis took the next exit and they sped down the off-ramp toward the main part of town. "Look at this place," she cried happily. "It's incredible."

"It's beautiful," Louis said quietly.

The lovely Spanish-influenced architecture of downtown Santa Fe created an old world atmosphere. The surrounding desert sand and turquoise blue of the sky were reflected in the stucco and tiles of the buildings.

Louis parked the car on a tree-lined side street. They got out of the car, stretching their stiff muscles. Up and down the winding road were art galleries and shops full of Native American crafts, artifacts, and paintings.

"It would be nice to live here," he commented. "But what would we do when we weren't *hanging out?*"

"Hanging out, if you do it right, takes up a lot of time," Jessica replied in a serious tone. "Of course, I know some people just hang out for an hour or two a day. Those people are *amateurs,*" she said in a voice heavy with disdain.

He laughed. "I think if we lived here, I'd paint."

"Why not?" Jessica said as they wandered into a gallery full of paintings. "Everybody else here seems to. There must be fifty art galleries on this street alone."

They walked slowly through the gallery, peering at figurative paintings of Native Americans. There were also abstract, colorful sculptures of things Jessica couldn't really identify. "I think if I were an artist, I would paint landscapes," she mused, looking out the window at the mountains behind the town. Nothing in the gallery matched the natural splendor of New Mexico.

"If I were an artist, I would paint you," he said, tugging at her hand.

They walked back into the bright afternoon sunlight and sauntered down the street. The air was warm, and Jessica wore her black sweater tied around her shoulders. The sleeves of her chambray shirt were rolled up to the elbow.

Jessica felt proud and happy as they passed other couples on the street. She wanted to lift their clasped hands and draw *everybody's* attention. After so much secrecy and fear, she was relieved to be out in the open and unafraid to display her affection for Louis.

They turned a corner and Jessica smiled. Native American vendors lined the sidewalk. Several people were selling beautiful sterling silver jewelry spread out on blankets. She and Louis strolled slowly along, looking and admiring the sculptural quality of the pendants and earrings.

An old Native American woman smiled at Jessica and her dark eyes twinkled. "Did you make all these?" Jessica asked. The pieces of silver jewelry laid out on the blanket were unusual and beautifully crafted. The woman nodded.

Suddenly Louis knelt to examine one of the pieces. His hand hovered over a pendant and closed. As Jessica watched Louis's quiet negotiation with the woman, she heard her laugh. He handed the vendor a generous amount of money and then stood, holding something in his hand.

He opened his fist and Jessica gasped. In his palm was a sterling silver unicorn on a chain. "For my lady," he said in a courtly voice.

The object was perfect. As a child, Jessica had belonged to a group of girls called the Unicorn Club. When she had told Miles about it, he had said he loved the idea of her with a unicorn. The image was right out of the medieval tapestries he lectured about in his history class.

Jessica swept her windblown blond hair up in her arms so that Louis could fasten the chain around her neck. She let her hair fall and took the mirror the lady offered. The pendant glowed in the hollow of her neck. "It's beautiful," she said. "I'll always wear it. Thank you."

He leaned over and kissed her cheek. "Thank *you*—for a perfect day."

"Waters!"

The company was assembled in the wooden ROTC headquarters building. They'd reached the end of a long, grueling day and the group laughed and joked as they stowed their gear in their lockers.

Lieutenant Drake motioned to her, and Denise followed him into a small inner office. He shut the door.

"Waters. We need to talk," he said sternly.

Denise straightened up a little and assumed the military listening posture—legs slightly straddled, hands behind her back, chin lifted, and eyes straight forward. "Sir. Yes, sir."

"Waters. You're a great recruit. A credit to the outfit."

"Thank you, sir."

"But Egbert is a mess. Since you're both new recruits and friends, I'm making you responsible for him."

"What!" she cried.

"I'm giving you a provisional promotion— which makes you Egbert's superior for the next few days. We're being inspected in three days by the top brass in the California ROTC program. The outcome of that inspection is going to affect whether or not I receive a promotion. I want that promotion, Waters. And that means I need every man and woman in this unit at one hundred percent military effectiveness. Waters, I want you to get Egbert up to speed in time for the inspection. And that's an order!"

"Sir. Yes, sir," she said in a subdued tone.

"That's all. You're dismissed."

Denise executed a crisp one-hundred-and-eighty-degree turn and marched out, torn between pity and rage. Why did Winston have to be such a hopeless klutz? And why did Lieutenant Drake pick her, of all people, to whip him into shape?

Chapter Nine

"Wow! Bruce said it wasn't romantic . . . but . . ." Todd broke off and laughed heartily. "This place is a dump."

Elizabeth looked around in appalled fascination. "I can't picture Lila Fowler living here."

"I can't picture *anybody* living here," Todd said, dropping their bags. "This place is unfit for human habitation."

"Well, we're going to have to inhabit it for now," Elizabeth said. "You want the bedroom or the sofa?"

"Doesn't matter to me," Todd said, poking his head in the kitchen. "Think you should call Tom and tell him where you are?"

Elizabeth glowered at Todd. "No. All I'll get is a big lecture about how if I'd listened to him, we wouldn't be in this predicament. But you should probably call Gin-Yung."

"If I call Gin-Yung," Todd retorted, "I'll get the same lecture. I don't want to hear it any more than you do."

"OK, OK," Elizabeth said. She flopped down on the sofa. "I'm going to the station. There's a laptop computer and a couple of boxes of files from the administration office there. I want to take a look through what's left and bring the laptop over here."

"Want me to go with you?" he asked.

She shook her head. "No. I'll probably attract less attention by myself and on foot. Later, though, I want to try talking to Daryl Cartright again. Of everybody we talked to, he knows the most."

Daryl Cartright was a former SVU basketball player. A high school star, he had not performed well at the college level last year. Eventually he had been dropped from the team, and shortly afterward he had left school. Elizabeth and Todd had tracked him down and discovered that he was one of the athletes involved in Santos's point-shaving operation. But he was adamant that he would never testify about his role in the illegal activity.

"He's also got the most to lose," Todd responded, plopping down in a chair and raising a cloud of dust.

Elizabeth shrugged. "I'm going to try anyway. What you said before was true. Most people are more comfortable telling the truth than they are lying. And Daryl Cartright's no different."

Todd nodded. "Yeah. But he's got a big invest-ment in lying."

Elizabeth stood and checked her pockets for her wallet, keys, and ID. "I'll call you from the station," she said, walking out the door.

"Be careful," he advised as she left.

Elizabeth jogged down the three flights of steps, thinking about Daryl Cartright. Todd was right—Daryl Cartright was in a tough spot. He knew what he was doing was wrong, but he didn't see any way out.

She could still picture him, tall, angry, and de-fensive, standing protectively between them and his home in the Hilldale housing project.

He'd come very close to breaking down then. He'd admitted that he had taken money to miss baskets, fix a few games, and then disappear from college athletics. But the people who had paid him were still sending money his way. Santos was foot-ing the bills for expensive doctors and treatments for Daryl's sister, Lucy. And he was making it pos-sible for Daryl to look after her and his two younger brothers.

Elizabeth thought this was a particularly ugly form of blackmail. Daryl hadn't been threatened; he'd been seduced. Seduced by the prospect of being able to provide his siblings with the things they needed. For Lucy, the need was medical treatment. For his brothers, it was Daryl's pres-ence on a daily basis.

Daryl Cartright had made it plain that he was

prepared to stand vigilant between his brothers, James and Pike, and the lure of gangs, drugs, guns, and crime. Even if protecting them involved taking money from someone as scummy and ruthless as T. Clay Santos.

Could Elizabeth possibly change his mind?

"My name is Tom Watts," Tom told the woman behind the desk. "I've been in the UBC conference all day, and I wondered if there are any messages for me."

The hotel employee smiled. "Which room?" she inquired pleasantly.

"Sixteen thirty," he responded, tapping his foot a little impatiently. Tom hadn't been able to get Elizabeth off his mind all day.

The concierge checked the wall of pigeonholes behind her and shook her head. "I'm sorry. There's nothing."

Tom bit his lip. "OK. Thanks." He shoved his hands in his pockets and walked around the lobby. Then he cut diagonally across the large room toward the phones.

He punched in Gin-Yung's number, and she answered immediately. "Hello?"

"Gin-Yung. It's Tom. I haven't been able to find Elizabeth all day. Do you have any idea what's going on?"

"Yes, I do." Her voice was low and angry.

"Something I should know about?" Tom said, feeling his heart sink a bit.

"Depends on who you ask. Elizabeth would probably say no."

"What does that mean?"

"Exactly what you think it means," Gin-Yung said fiercely.

Tom gripped the phone in frustration. Apparently something *was* going on between Todd and Elizabeth. If Gin-Yung was right, how serious was the rekindled spark? Tom wanted nothing more than to go get on a plane and head back to Sweet Valley University. But he couldn't. He had a professional obligation to stay in Las Vegas. The debut cable event was one of the biggest things ever planned on the Sweet Valley University campus. The wrestling match wasn't taking place until the day after tomorrow, and Tom absolutely had to stay to cover it.

"Gin-Yung, what are you going to do?" Tom asked.

"I'm not sure. But we will, of course, keep you informed as this story develops," she said in an ironic tone before abruptly hanging up.

"Mmmmm." Lila's sharp white teeth pulled the chicken from the bone, and she chewed with relish. Nothing had ever tasted quite as good.

"This casserole is great stuff," Bruce said enthusiastically, pointing to his plate with his fork.

Lila nodded. "That's Hannah's secret recipe. Artichokes and mushrooms with some kind of seasoning. Don't ask me what it is. She won't tell."

Bruce took another big bite and reached for a roll. "Whatever it is, I'm in heaven."

Mr. and Mrs. Fowler had been out when they arrived, and Lila had led Bruce directly to the kitchen of Fowler Crest. The room was huge, with restaurant-size refrigerators and dishwashers, and as lavish and ornate as the rest of the house. Bright copper pans hung from the ceiling, and colorful French tiles lined the walls. Behind them was an open fireplace.

Lila's parents entertained often, and there was almost always plenty of party food left in the refrigerator. Starving, Bruce and Lila had pulled out container after container of food. They'd arranged the dishes in a line on the large, highly polished wooden kitchen table. The setup was their own personal smorgasbord.

"Mmmmm," Bruce murmured appreciatively. "This is like being turned loose in the kitchen of a five-star restaurant."

So far they'd eaten leftover prime rib with horseradish, warmed in the microwave. Lila had feasted on cold, breaded chicken strips with a Dijon mustard sauce while Bruce was gorging on a dish of chicken-and-artichoke casserole that was delicious served hot or cold. They'd discovered a vegetable terrine was to die for. And on a silver dish sat a mold of something rich and a tart made with cream cheese and dill.

Lila helped herself to a slice of thick chocolate mousse cake. "Bruce," she began, tentatively broaching a subject that had been on her mind ever since they'd walked into the mansion. "Instead of going back home tonight, what would you think about staying here?"

"Here, in your house? With your parents? Both of us?" He looked vaguely alarmed.

"No!" she said quickly. "I mean, I'll stay here, and you go stay at your house."

Bruce looked relieved. "Yeah. That's a good idea. My parents would be happy to see me. I haven't been home in a while."

Lila smiled, feeling as if a huge weight had been lifted from her shoulders. She didn't know how to tell him, but Bruce was getting on her nerves in a major way. She desperately needed a little privacy break.

The problem wasn't so much that he actually did anything *wrong*. Well, actually, yes, he did do a lot of things wrong. But it was little things that bugged her. For one, he kept forgetting to put the seat down on the toilet. And he cleared his throat too often. She'd noticed that he insisted on squeezing the toothpaste tube in the middle instead of from the bottom. He washed his hands at least every three minutes. He cracked his knuckles. He even smiled all the time.

Suddenly all Lila wanted was for Bruce to be gone.

He looked at his watch. "Actually, Lila, I think I'll go on home now—if you don't mind. My mom and dad should be home from work and . . ."

"Oh, go on," she said graciously.

"I feel like I should stay until your parents get home and at least say hello." Even as Bruce said the words, he was edging toward the kitchen door.

"Don't be silly," she said. "I'm fine here."

"I could wait," he said.

"No!" Lila snapped. "Leave now."

His eyes widened.

"I mean, don't feel like you have to stay and be polite," she said in a softer tone. "You can talk to my folks tomorrow when you pick me up."

Bruce smiled—the big wide-smile that irritated her to death. "OK. If you're sure."

That was another thing that was bothering her. His constant need to be reassured on every single point. Funny, she'd always thought of Bruce as being very confident. Very self-possessed. Almost an egomaniac. Now she saw him as somewhat diffident and altogether too worried about what she thought.

He smiled and nervously wiped his hands. "Well," he said. "See you tomorrow."

"See you tomorrow," she echoed, getting quickly to her feet. She took his arm and walked him to the front hall, fighting the impulse to shove him out the door.

Bruce went down the front steps of the Fowler mansion feeling like a man who had just made a very narrow escape. Jeez! He'd never been so glad to be by himself.

Ever since he and Lila had started talking about living together, he'd felt himself turning into a completely different person. He was used to thinking only about his own comfort. But he knew that if he was going to be successful at living with Lila, he was going to have to try to be sensitive to her feelings.

But his attempts to ingratiate himself just seemed to irritate her. And Lila could be really bad tempered sometimes. He climbed into his car and sighed deeply. He was looking forward to the peace and quiet of his own room. He reached for his car phone and dialed the apartment to tell Todd and Elizabeth to make themselves at home. He and Lila wouldn't be back tonight.

Elizabeth felt a tendril of hair escaping from underneath her baseball cap. She tucked it back up with her thumb and adjusted her large dark sunglasses.

The late-afternoon sun was shining directly onto her head, and she felt slightly dizzy. She was walking down the street toward the campus when she saw two large figures silhouetted in the sun. They were walking in her direction. She squinted through the glare and realized that one of them was Bobbo.

She could tell that he spotted her at the same moment she recognized him. Elizabeth backed up, turned, and began running. The baseball cap flew off and her long hair streamed out behind her.

Two guys coming out of a pastry shop almost fell backward in surprise when she whipped between them, ran into the shop, and looked around frantically. A shocked clerk in a paper hat and white jacket watched her from behind the cash register. "Is there a back door?" she demanded.

He nodded and gestured over his shoulder, beginning to sputter a question. Without waiting to hear what he had to say, Elizabeth vaulted over the counter, disappeared into the back, and fought her way in the dark past the stacks of cardboard boxes containing supplies.

Groping around, she found the back door and her hands pushed the metal bar. The thick door opened onto a back alley lined with trash cans and discarded crates. Her sneakers made no noise as she ran along the pavement. But a few seconds later, she heard the clatter of men's shoes behind her.

She glanced over her shoulder and saw Bobbo and his sidekick closing in. Elizabeth was surprised at how fast he moved, considering how big he was. He must have played football. A light went on in her head. Santos's business was corrupting athletes. She just hoped the other guy wasn't a former track-and-field star.

Another glance over her shoulder confirmed her fears. Bobbo's sidekick had lowered his head and was sprinting after her, closing the distance between them like an all-star.

She emerged from the alley, turned right, and

ran down the boulevard that separated the shopping district from the north side of the campus. A car came around the corner and began accelerating toward her as she crossed the street at a diagonal. The vehicle came within inches of hitting her before skidding to a stop with a squeal of its tires. A familiar head poked out of the driver's-side window. "Get in!" Gin-Yung ordered.

Elizabeth wildly made her way to the passenger side, wrenched open the door, and fell into the car as Gin-Yung pounded the gas pedal with her small foot.

The car lurched forward and Elizabeth straightened up and looked out the back window. Bobbo and his friend stood in the street, watching the car speed away.

"Thanks," she said, smiling at Gin-Yung.

"Don't thank me yet," Gin-Yung said sourly. The car careened around another corner at top speed before Gin-Yung pulled into a parking place along the shop-lined street and slammed on the brakes. "OK," she said, turning to face Elizabeth. "What's going on with you and Todd?"

Elizabeth couldn't help smiling. Gin-Yung looked almost as angry and formidable as Chloe or Mr. Santos. "Nothing," she assured her.

"That's a lie," Gin-Yung accused tearfully. "I've been calling Todd all day, and he doesn't answer. I saw you guys together at the gas station . . . you two looked pretty steamy."

Elizabeth groaned. "Gin-Yung! That was an act."

"An act?"

As quickly as possible, Elizabeth filled Gin-Yung in on what had happened to her and Todd since yesterday. She explained that she and Todd had had to behave like a couple needing a little time alone in order to wrangle the use of the apartment from Bruce and Lila.

"So Bruce and Lila are there with you?" Gin-Yung asked.

"Well," Elizabeth hedged. "Not exactly. They went home."

Gin-Yung looked skeptical. "So you and Todd are staying together at Lila and Bruce's apartment—all by yourselves?"

"Just until it's safe to come out of hiding," Elizabeth assured her.

"How long will that be?" Gin-Yung asked, frowning.

Elizabeth ran her hands through her hair and massaged her scalp. "I don't know," she admitted wearily. "I feel like we've hit a wall."

"Then let me help you," Gin-Yung said. "Stop picking my brains for information and then giving me the big kiss-off."

"Hey! I've wanted your help all along. But Todd's worried that we're in too much danger."

"I'll talk to Todd," Gin-Yung said. "And if you don't mind, I'd like to talk to him alone."

Elizabeth smiled. "Fine with me."

"So where is this apartment?"

Elizabeth laughed. "What's it worth to you to know?"

"Come on, Elizabeth," Gin-Yung said, pounding her fist on the steering wheel. "Play straight with me."

"OK, OK. Don't get mad. I just want to know if I can borrow your car."

"What for?"

"I need to go talk to Daryl Cartright. At this point, he's pretty much our last hope. If he won't talk, Todd and I may be stuck in Bruce and Lila's fleabag apartment for the rest of our lives."

Todd was filling the teakettle with water when he heard the door slam. "Elizabeth, do you want some tea?"

"No. I don't want any tea," said an altogether unexpected voice.

Todd came out of the kitchen. Gin-Yung stood in the doorway, peering at him from beneath her silky black bangs. "I'm in this investigation, and I'm staying in. I don't care what you say."

"Well. I'm certainly glad we had a chance to thoroughly thrash things out and discuss it," Todd said sarcastically.

"Just tell me this. Have you still got a thing for Elizabeth?"

Todd put the kettle down on the stove and walked toward her with his arms open. "Gin-Yung," he whispered, gathering her up in his arms and laying his cheek against the top of her head. "I've got a thing for you. In fact, I've got it so bad that even though I know I should be furious at you for pushing your way into a dangerous situation, I'm incredibly glad you're here." He kissed her softly. "Because being away from you gets harder and harder every day."

Her small body felt like a bird in his arms. And when she kissed him, her delicate lips sent butterflies racing up his spine. Todd sighed, feeling content for the first time in days. With Gin-Yung by his side, he could handle anything.

"You again?"

"It's a good thing I'm not sensitive," Elizabeth said wryly. "Otherwise I might get the impression you're not happy to see me."

Daryl Cartright looked anything but happy to see her. He stood inside his house, regarding her from behind his screen door—which remained conspicuously closed. "I thought I told you not to come back," he said bluntly.

"I need to talk to you. If I could just have a few minutes . . ." She looked at him, her eyes pleading.

"I told you before. I've got nothing to say." Daryl was over six-three. With his short red hair and baggy shorts and T-shirt, he looked pretty formidable. Elizabeth wouldn't be able to push past him, and he clearly didn't plan on moving to let her step into the house.

When a tiny figure maneuvered around Daryl's legs, Elizabeth looked down and smiled. Lucy, Daryl's little sister, was grinning up at her.

"Hi," she said in a bright voice. "I remember you." She swung open the door, and Elizabeth moved to the top of the front steps.

"I remember you too," Elizabeth said, kneeling down. "How are you, Lucy?"

"I'm fine." Lucy settled herself more comfortably on her crutches, and Daryl put a hand on her shoulder to steady her. The evening was warm, and Lucy wore a little blue-and-yellow dress covered with a sunflower pattern. She still had steel braces on her legs and heavy corrective shoes on her feet, but Elizabeth noticed that the shoelaces were bright yellow.

"Neat shoelaces," Elizabeth said.

"Daryl got them," Lucy explained. She shot a look up at her brother. "Can Elizabeth stay for dinner?"

Elizabeth couldn't help smiling. Lucy was putting her big brother on the spot. He clearly wanted to tell Elizabeth to bug off, but Lucy's sunny disposition and cordial welcome was making it impossible for him to be rude.

"I'm really hungry," Elizabeth said. "You're not by any chance making spaghetti again?"

"Meat loaf," Lucy answered. She tugged on the hem of Daryl's shorts. "Invite her," she urged in a stage whisper.

"Would you like to stay for dinner?" he asked in a grudging voice.

"I'd love to," Elizabeth said cheerfully, ignoring the complete lack of enthusiasm in his voice.

Daryl backed up so that Elizabeth could come

inside. Then she followed him and Lucy into the kitchen. Two younger boys sat at the kitchen table, eyeing her with curiosity. One boy was about ten years old. The other was taller, and at first Elizabeth thought he was almost Daryl's age. But a closer look at his face made her realize he was young—probably only twelve or thirteen.

They stood politely, and Daryl made the introductions. "These are my brothers, James and Pike. Boys, this is Elizabeth Wakefield. She's a friend from school."

James gave her a shy smile, and Pike gave her a wide grin. "Hi," he said. "Do you go to college?"

"That's right," Elizabeth answered. "I'm a freshman."

"I'm going to go to college," Pike announced proudly. "Just like Daryl. I'm going to get a basketball scholarship."

"He's good," Lucy said sagely. "We think he can do it."

Elizabeth turned toward Daryl, and he nodded. "He's got the moves," he said. "I've been working with him, and I think he's got a really good chance for a scholarship." The praise was understated, but the look on his face told Elizabeth that Daryl was enormously pleased with Pike.

Daryl walked over to James and put his arm around his youngest brother's shoulders. "James here is going to go to college too. He's not very athletic, but his teachers say he's sure to get a scholarship. He's a straight-A student."

"Wow!" Elizabeth said. "This is an impressive family."

A buzzer on the oven went off. Suddenly everybody was in motion at once. "Sit here," Lucy ordered while Daryl began unloading dishes from the oven. The boys scrambled around to set another place at the table.

The plates and glasses were mismatched. But there was a clean tablecloth and the kitchen had a festive, family feeling that belied the depressing atmosphere outside the cheerful home.

Daryl put the meat loaf on the table, and James brought a bowl of salad over from the counter. James helped Lucy into her chair and then stood politely behind Elizabeth's chair until she was seated. "Thank you," she said.

Clearly the Cartright family thought manners were important. She glanced at Daryl. His face was a mixture of pride in his family and resentment at her intrusion. She knew he was coping with a difficult situation. His parents were both dead, and he was trying to be mother and father to two brothers and a sister with a very complicated set of needs.

"Tell me what you want to do when you grow up," Elizabeth said to Lucy.

"I'm going to be a doctor," Lucy answered.

"Me too," James said.

"We're both going to be doctors," Lucy said. "We're going to have an office together." She grinned at her brother and wiggled in excitement.

"Pike thinks we should be sports medicine doctors."

"You should," Pike said, reaching for a piece of bread. "That way if I bust up my knee or something, you can fix it for me."

"You'll never get hurt," James said, buttering his bread. "You're too fast."

Daryl knocked on the table. "Don't say things like that. It's bad luck." His eyes looked momentarily troubled.

"I *am* fast," Pike said proudly. He turned to Elizabeth. "I'm the fastest guy on the team at school. My coach says I'm definitely going to the pros." He passed the salad to Daryl. "Coach told me again today that you were the best player he ever had."

Daryl smiled. "Until you."

"Well." Pike grinned modestly. "He didn't say that."

"He should. You're twice as good as I was when I was your age. You'll get to the pros." He put down the salad and gave Pike a significant look. "If you keep your nose clean between now and then."

Daryl cared a lot about these kids, Elizabeth thought. He was trying to give them a future. And he had done it by sacrificing his own. Elizabeth put a forkful of meat loaf in her mouth and was pleasantly surprised. "This is good!" she said in amazement.

Daryl smiled slowly. "Didn't think I could cook, did you?"

"Well," Elizabeth said, buttering her own piece of bread. "It's not you. I've just had a lifelong suspicion of meat loaf. You never know exactly what's in it."

The comment prompted the two boys to launch into horror stories about the food in their own school cafeterias. Lucy giggled along and for the next half hour, the group of four laughed and joked while they ate.

Finally the meat loaf was gone and everybody insisted that Elizabeth finish the last scrap of salad, which she did with pleasure. "Daryl, I think maybe you've got a future cooking."

While the kids cleared the table and did the dishes, Elizabeth caught Daryl's eye and jerked her head toward the living room.

"Excuse us," Daryl said to his siblings. "We're going to sit in the living room and talk. Can you guys handle the cleanup on your own?"

When they insisted they had the kitchen under control, Elizabeth followed Daryl into the living room and sat in the chair that he indicated. "Look," he said. "I don't mean to seem unfriendly. And I know you don't think much of me. But . . ."

"You're wrong. I have a lot of respect for you," Elizabeth interrupted. "That's why I keep coming back. I don't blame you for being unfriendly. You've done what you thought you had to do." She nodded toward the kitchen. "What do they know?"

"Nothing," Daryl said emphatically. "Just that I didn't do too well, got bumped from the team, and that was it for me and college."

Elizabeth bit her lip. "You have a lot of dreams for Pike, don't you?"

"I've got dreams for all of them. But Pike's the one who's the most like me. If I can keep him on the straight and narrow for just a couple more years, he's got a chance to have all the stuff I didn't get. A college education. NCAA exposure. A shot at the pros. Sports could be his ticket. And a ticket out for James and Lucy, too. Medical school is expensive. Pro ball pays big money. And if he doesn't end up with a career in basketball, at least he'll have a college degree. He can help James and Lucy, and he will. If he can, he'll see to it that they get educations."

Elizabeth nodded and shot him a look. "And what happens when somebody comes along and offers *him* money to drop the ball?"

Daryl's head jerked up. "What?"

"What if somebody says to him, 'Pike, you've got a brother and sister who want to go to medical school. Medical school is expensive, and we're going to offer you a way to pay for it.'" Elizabeth paused. "You said Pike is the most like you of all the kids. And he'll probably do exactly what you did if he thinks he can get James and Lucy the things they need."

Daryl stared at her, his expressive eyes reflecting alarm as the truth of her observation sank in.

116

Louis handed the classical guitar player a couple of dollars and whispered his request. The musician nodded and smiled while Louis returned to the table.

He and Jessica sat on the second-floor balcony of a restaurant. The desert view was one of the most spectacular Louis had ever seen. Now they had finished their dinner and were lingering over coffee as the sun concluded its descent in the sky.

Louis reached across the table for Jessica's hand as the guitarist began plucking the familiar chords Louis had requested. "This is a pretty melody," she said softly. "What is it?"

"A fifteenth-century ballad," he answered. "A song of love." He laced his fingers around hers and admired her hand. Like the rest of Jessica, her hand was graceful and feminine.

"How did you get interested in medieval history?" she asked suddenly.

He laughed. "Those years constitute a fascinating period of history. The age is exciting to study—but more than anything else, it's romantic."

She smiled. "You're not like any other man I've known."

"How am I different?"

Jessica's eyes twinkled. "Well, I was going to say you were romantic. But that's not it. Lots of guys have been romantic. You're . . . chivalrous," she said, finding the right word.

"I take that as a very high compliment," he said solemnly.

"I never really understood what that meant before." She gazed at their hands, her eyes thoughtful. "But now I realize that to some extent, chivalry is another word for the kind of love that matters. A willingness to put someone else's happiness first."

Louis stared at her hand again. "You make me feel like a fraud, Jessica. A truly chivalrous man would have put your safety above every other concern. I would never have formed any attachment to you. Or let you form one to me. Because I knew that Chloe . . ."

She leaned across the table and put her finger to his lips. "First of all, the sun hasn't set yet. Second, I didn't *form an attachment*. I fell in love with you. And that's different. We belong together—no matter what."

He glanced out over the balcony. "Unfortunately, Cinderella, the sun *is* disappearing as we speak." He released her hand and leaned back, feeling a restless and fearful stir in the pit of his stomach. "We've stayed a long time in one place. It's time to move on. We'll drive all night."

He saw her fingers fly to the unicorn. She touched the necklace as if it were a talisman. He reached out to caress the hand that still lay on the table. She was *his* talisman. Jessica gave him courage and even hope. She was a reason to keep moving. To keep running.

He stood, took her blue jean jacket from the back of her chair, and held it for her to put on. "It's getting cold," he said, helping her on with the jacket when she stood.

Louis put his arm around her, and they descended the stone stairs built along the vine-covered outside wall of the restaurant. Hand in hand, they began walking down the street toward his car. Above their heads, the night sky held one last brilliant streak of pink.

The landscape was beautiful in a way that made his soul ache. Beautiful in a way that was sad and haunting. Because sunsets only lasted for a brief few moments. And when they were over, everything was dark.

They climbed in the car, and he leaned over and opened the glove compartment, looking for his watch. It was gone. And so was Jessica's makeup bag. "Oh no," he whispered hoarsely. He looked quickly in the backseat and locked the doors. "Put on your seat belt," he ordered.

"What is it? What's the matter?" Jessica fumbled quickly for her seat belt.

"Somebody's been in the car. My watch is gone, and so is your makeup." He backed out with a squeal of tires.

"Louis," she cried. "Be careful."

When he gunned the engine, she pulled at his sleeve. "You're overreacting. It can't be Chloe. It was just some thief. Slow down."

Louis took some deep breaths. Was she right? It was possible. People popped locks and rifled glove compartments all the time. Maybe some kid had broken into the car on a dare. Or maybe a petty thief had thought he could get some money for Louis's watch.

Still, there was no sense in taking any chances. He glanced in the rearview mirror and got on the highway, heading for Colorado.

"Elizabeth needs to call Tom," Gin-Yung said to Todd. "And by the way, that disguise looks totally stupid. I would recognize you from a mile away."

Todd laughed and adjusted the bandanna on his head. "What? I don't look like a grunge musician?"

"No. You look like an all-American ex–basketball player with a red bandanna on his head."

They were walking toward the campus on their

way to the newspaper office. When they reached one of the many construction sites, Todd suddenly gripped Gin-Yung's hand. "Look at that truck."

Gin-Yung scrutinized the white van parked beside the curb. "Just looks like an average truck to me."

"Yeah, but there seem to be a lot of them around campus. And Santos's henchmen were in a truck like that this morning."

Gin-Yung reached into the pocket of her navy-blue blazer and pulled out a pad and a stub of pencil, jotting down the license plate number.

Todd glanced nervously around to see if Bobbo or any of Bobbo's clones were hanging around the site. But there were no workmen to be seen. Todd frowned. "You know, all this renovation started weeks ago, and I've never noticed any workmen. Have you?"

Gin-Yung shook her head. "No. But that's not surprising. You know how hard it is to get a good construction crew." She put the pad back in her jacket. "Let's just get to the newspaper office and try to reconstruct the information I gave you and Liz. I've got a friend who works the night shift at the police department. If it'll make you feel better, we can run the plates and see who owns the truck." She took his hand and pulled him toward the student union building. "Let's go down into the snack lounge and get some food to take with us."

"OK," he agreed. "But keep your eyes peeled for trouble."

A few moments later they were entering the student union. To the right, through heavy glass doors, was the cafeteria, which was closed.

To the left was the enormous student activities hall. The room was used for dances, registration, and other special events that required a large space.

Even though it was late, student tech crews were busily rushing in and out of the hall, carrying large monitors on dollies. "I guess they're getting ready for the broadcast of the wrestling match," Todd commented. "Come on. Let's go in and look around."

They went through the doors and Gin-Yung whistled. "Wow! Check out this setup." Ten enormous big-screen TVs were mounted high on the walls surrounding the room. There was a podium with a microphone where Dr. Beal would get up, announce the premiere event of the new all-NCAA sports channel, and probably say a few words about how proud they were that SVU's star wrestler, Craig Maser, had been chosen to be a part of the broadcast.

"They ought to be able to get at least four hundred people in here," Todd said. "Tom did a good job getting the arrangements made before he left."

"Speaking of Tom . . ." Gin-Yung said. "Elizabeth really should call him. I think he's as suspicious as I was."

"You tell Elizabeth," Todd said with a laugh.

"I'm through telling anybody anything. Come on. Let's get some coffee and hit the newspaper office."

Winston tossed and turned on his bed. It was late and his body was exhausted. But his mind kept spinning. The day had been the most awful of his whole life. He had embarrassed himself and, more important, embarrassed Denise to the extent that she didn't even want to admit that he was her boyfriend.

He wondered what happened to people who resigned from the ROTC. Did he have that option? He didn't think he did.

So what happened to people who went absent without leave? Did the military police hunt down AWOLs like dogs? Did they drum them out into the center of the field and snip off their buttons with a lot of pomp and circumstance? Was the military still allowed to hang people?

Winston groaned out loud and ground his teeth. "I'll never cheat again," he vowed out loud, remembering his ill-fated physics test. "Never."

Denise stared out her window at the stars in the sky. She'd never felt so unhappy. She was deeply ashamed about the way she had treated Winston today.

But at the same time, she had a tremendous amount of anger. Why couldn't he behave appropriately just once? Why did he have to humiliate her?

She had always been proud of Winston's wit and ability to make people laugh. But the ROTC wasn't the place for jokes and clowning around. Military training provided an opportunity to get serious about mental and physical fitness. If Winston wanted to be her boyfriend, he was going to have to shape up.

Denise turned away from the window with her mind made up. She crossed the door with purpose in her step. She needed to talk to Winston. Immediately.

Down the hall, she pounded on Winston's door. "Winston. Get up."

There was a long pause, and then she heard his footsteps crossing the room. He opened the door a crack. "What do you want?"

She put her hand on the door and pushed it open, walking in. "I've got to tell you something."

"What?" he asked sullenly.

"I got promoted this afternoon. As of now, I'm your superior officer."

Winston put his index finger in his mouth, popped it against his cheek, and then circled it in the air. "Well, whoop-de-do!"

Denise stared at him, her lip trembling. Clearly he was hurt and upset, but he didn't have to be sarcastic. "Listen, Winston. I only joined this stupid ROTC to be with you. Neither one of us would even be here if you hadn't cheated on that test."

He flinched as if he had been slapped. "Hey!

Listen. I know you're ashamed of me. You've made that obvious. You don't have to keep going over and over it."

"Yes, I am ashamed of you," she shouted. "But not because you cheated. And not because you can't march or twirl a gun. I'm ashamed because you won't *try,* and then you make a joke out of it."

"What good does it do to try?" he demanded. "I'll never be any good at this kind of stuff. If you want a guy who's good at parading around like a soldier, go out with the real thing—Lieutenant Drake."

Denise felt a rush of color in her cheeks, and Winston's jaw dropped. "That's it, isn't it? You like him now. Right?"

"I respect him," she answered in a terse voice. "And he wants me to work with you and get you up to speed in time for the inspection. So meet me on the drill field at six A.M."

"What if I say no?"

"Winston," she repeated in flat voice. "Meet me at six A.M. on the drill field. And that's an *order.*"

"And if I disobey, what happens?"

Denise felt herself shaking. This was the first time she had ever seen Winston look at her with anything but love and slavish adoration. As angry as she felt, she had a sudden and overwhelming sense of loss.

The look in his eyes wasn't loving or adoring. It was openly hostile. He wasn't going to let her push him around anymore. He wasn't hers for the asking. He wasn't her devotee.

But he *was* her subordinate. "If you don't, Lieutenant Drake will inform the disciplinary council that you are uncooperative. And I guess you'll be expelled." Her lip was trembling, but she wasn't going to let him see her cry. "See you at six," she said shortly, turning away and striding down the hall to her own room. She heard his door slam shut behind her.

Louis blinked, fighting to keep his eyes open. He flexed his fingers, realizing that they were stiff from gripping the steering wheel all night. So far, they'd stuck to the main highways. If Chloe were behind them, she would have had plenty of time to catch up.

Spending the day in Santa Fe had been wonderful. But it had been an insane thing to do. They had lost time, valuable time.

Chloe was a relentless predator, and he felt compelled now to keep moving. He had to make up for the lost time.

Louis slowed the car as they approached the city limits of a small town. There wasn't a soul on the street. The town square had such a sleepy, peaceful feeling that he felt almost foolish stopping at the red light.

He glanced down at Jessica. She lay with her

head on his shoulder and her jacket pulled around her for warmth. He drummed his fingers on the wheel. Exhaustion was setting in and making him feel restless.

When the light changed, he pressed the gas, pulling past the closed shops—a pharmacy, an auto-parts store, a garage, a ladies' clothing store. The town seemed so simple, so safe. He blinked again, this time fighting tears. If only they could stop. Stop and rest and just be together. Marry. Work. Play. Have friends. Children. He smiled, picturing a little blond daughter with Jessica's spark and humor.

He passed a quiet intersection and noticed a black Mazda parked beneath a streetlamp. As his own car slowly moved past the intersection, the lights on the Mazda turned on and the car pulled out onto the road.

His heart began to thump wildly. Could it be?

No, he thought, forcing himself to be rational. There were a million black Mazdas on the road. This didn't mean a thing. He glanced at Jessica, making sure she was asleep, then he glanced again in the rearview mirror. There was nothing behind him but darkness as they left the little town and its peacefully sleeping residents far behind.

I need coffee, he thought, pressing his foot against the gas. He was getting dangerously tired and wondered if he was possibly hallucinating.

When he passed the last house on the outskirts of town, he pressed the pedal harder, letting the engine roar. There would be a diner or truck stop somewhere.

Jessica felt the roar of the engine as the car lurched forward. She blinked and sat up. They were flying along the highway, and Louis's hands were tight on the wheel. His eyes were hard and intent on the road.

"Is something wrong?" she asked.

Louis shook his head but didn't answer.

She put her hand on his knee. "Are you tired?"

"Yes," he said in a tight voice. "I am. We'll stop and get some coffee. OK with you?"

"Fine with me," she said. She yawned and sat up, stretching the muscles in her neck and back. "Want me to drive?"

He glanced in the rearview mirror and chewed his lip thoughtfully. "Not yet. Maybe in a bit."

"Are you sure nothing's wrong?" she asked, noting the set of his head and the edge in his voice.

"I don't think so." He gave her an exhausted but reassuring smile. "I'm just tense. I've been awake a long time. I'll get some coffee, and I'll be fine."

"You need to sleep," Jessica said. "Let's find someplace to stop."

"We will," he promised. "But not yet. Aha! Look!" They passed a billboard that announced a twenty-four-hour diner off the next exit.

Louis turned the wheel and they flew off the

exit, too fast. Jessica's fingers gripped the edge of her seat. Minutes later Louis pulled into a parking space and looked carefully around before he unlocked the door. There were no other cars in the parking lot. Through the window they could see that the diner was empty except for one waitress who sat at the counter, reading the paper and smoking a cigarette.

He unlocked the doors, and they got out of the car and stretched. Louis walked ahead toward the diner while Jessica paused, adjusting the sock in her boot.

Jessica heard the car before she saw it. The high-pitched whine of an engine made her look up. Suddenly, from out of nowhere, a car was bearing down on her.

"Jessica!" Louis yelled. "Look out!"

Jessica threw herself toward Louis's car, rolling over the trunk just as the black Mazda raced through the parking lot at seventy-five miles per hour.

The noise attracted the attention of the waitress, and Jessica caught a glimpse of her running to the pay phone on the wall of the diner.

Several yards away the Mazda was circling, preparing to make another pass.

Louis ran back toward the car, opened the door, and thrust Jessica inside. He practically fell in on top of her. "Put on your seat belt," he ordered as she struggled to the passenger side.

He backed the car out just as the Mazda came

careening toward them. His foot floored the pedal, and they shot backward toward the diner.

The Mazda missed them by inches and the back of Louis's Toyota shattered the plate glass of the diner window. He jammed the car into drive and hit the pedal again, taking off with so much velocity that the car actually went airborne as they pulled out of the parking lot, heading for the highway feeder.

Jessica turned and looked over the back of the seat. The Mazda had made too sharp a turn and was in a spin in the parking lot. She held her breath, waiting for the car to careen into a lamppost. But the driver pulled out of the skid just in time. The Mazda came roaring onto the feeder behind them.

The sound of police sirens filled the air. Jessica watched the black Mazda make a crazy U-turn, cut its lights, and fade into the night.

Louis turned out his own headlights. "We don't want to get mixed up with the police," he said, racing up the ramp and onto the dark highway that led out of town. "We'll head north, toward the mountains." It was easy to get lost up there. Easy to hide.

"Can't we stop?" Jessica begged, her heart pounding and her hands shaking. "If the police are coming, maybe they can help us."

He shook his head. "No, they won't. They'll try. But they'll want us to stay in the area, and the minute we stop moving . . ." He trailed off and didn't finish.

Jessica tightened her seat belt and clasped her hands nervously together. She knew what he was going to say. Chloe was dangerous. And by the time the police figured out just how dangerous, it might be too late.

She glanced at Louis's face. The carefree, happy expression she had seen during their one perfect day was completely gone. The young and charming Professor Miles had evaporated. In his stead there was a tense, angry, and desperate man.

"In another ten miles, we can exit onto some side roads. She'll have a harder time picking up our trail if we stay off the main highways for a while."

Jessica nodded, but she remained silent. A weight pressed at her shoulders and a heavy feeling settled in her stomach. Chloe would hound them to the ends of the earth. She was relentless— this nightmarish journey was never going to end.

"I've stolen your life from you," he said. His lips moved silently, as if he had no words to describe the enormity of the situation. "This kind of existence is living death. You might as well be dead. You're cut off from your family. You're cut off from your friends."

She understood what he meant now. Life on the run was a kind of living death. But she didn't care. Because in life or in death, all she wanted was to be with Louis. He was her knight. And she was his lady. For luck she kissed her fingertips, then pressed them to the silver unicorn.

*   *   *

Todd squinted, poring over the long printouts that Gin-Yung had generated from the computer banks at the newspaper office. The office was located in the basement of the language arts building, and Gin-Yung spent almost as much time there as Elizabeth and Tom spent at the TV station. The yearly budgets for previous years were easily accessed via the university mainframe. Now he and Gin-Yung were hoping to find some of the information that had been lost in Elizabeth's computer.

The phone rang, and Gin-Yung grabbed it. *"Gazette!"* She broke into a huge smile and waved at Todd to pay attention. "Hey, Grouper. What have you got?" She grabbed a pencil and paper, then scribbled a few notes. "You're kidding."

"What's going on?" he mouthed to Gin-Yung. She put one hand over his mouth, signaling him to be quiet. "So how many other plates are registered to the same company?" She made another notation. "OK, Grouper. Thanks a million. You got it. Two seats to the next SVU tennis match." She hung up the phone and turned a shining face toward Todd. "That was my friend at the police station. Guess who that truck was registered to?"

Todd took a sip of his cold coffee and shrugged. "No-Show Construction?"

"Got it in one."

"Huh?"

"The plates are registered to TCS Construction."

"So?"

Gin-Yung glared at him. "You know, I guess I should be grateful you're not planning to make a career out of espionage."

He laughed. "Hey! I'm tired. We've been here practically all night. Tell me what you're getting at."

"TCS Construction. *T. Clay Santos* Construction."

Todd felt a lightbulb go off in his head. He put down the coffee cup and waved the printouts. "Do you have any idea how many payments there are here to TCS Construction?"

"I'm going to bet a lot."

Todd began to pace. "This doesn't prove anything, though. I mean, so Santos is in the construction business. There's nothing illegal about the school using him to do their construction."

"*If* he's doing the construction. Which, from the look of the sites, I don't think he is."

Todd sat back and narrowed his eyes, thinking. Off the top of his head, he could think of five construction areas around campus that seemed abandoned, untended, and unfinished.

"Look. They've got a perfect way to launder gambling money," Gin-Yung said. "Gamblers posing as alum donate dirty money. The money filters through the various university budgets and gets paid out to a construction company for work that either never gets done or gets overcharged for."

"But how do we *prove* it?" Todd asked.

Gin-Yung bit her lip. "I don't know. It's still

speculation. And the evidence is largely circumstantial."

"So we're right back where we started." Todd sighed. "We need a witness."

Outside, they heard the screech of tires. Gin-Yung dragged a chair over to the window, stood on it, and looked out the high basement window. "Uh-oh. I think we've got company." She turned out the lights, and Todd came over and climbed up beside her.

A gray sedan had pulled up outside. Two large men climbed out. They were wearing ski masks.

"I think we'd better get out of here," Gin-Yung said quietly. She hopped off the chair and moved it back to the desk. She grabbed the computer printout, opened the drawer, and took out a cellular phone. "It's mine," she explained. "I use the phone sometimes to call in my column from away games. You never know when it'll come in handy."

"Come on." Todd took her hand, and they moved silently toward the window on the other side of the room. It, too, was high up on the wall.

"How did they find us?" she asked.

"Maybe the phones here are tapped," Todd speculated.

"Sure," Gin-Yung said grimly. "Why not? Tapping a phone is the easiest thing in the world. The phones are probably tapped at the TV station, too."

"Here they come," Todd said. "Let's get ready

to run." He boosted Gin-Yung up and through the window. Then he chinned himself up, climbing over the ledge and pulling the window shut behind him as he climbed out onto the ground outside.

From inside the office, they could hear the sound of the door bursting open and equipment being smashed to bits.

"You'd better hide out with me and Elizabeth tonight," Todd said, taking her hand and starting to run.

"You want me to spend the night in that dump?" she joked.

"Hey! If it's good enough for Lila Fowler and Bruce Patman, it ought to be good enough for us."

Hand in hand, they ran in silence toward his car, which was parked on a back street. Todd felt oddly elated. Not since William White had tried to murder him and everybody he knew had he been in so much danger. But somehow, he was having a good time. Because this time, he wasn't in danger alone. He had Elizabeth on his side. And best of all, he had Gin-Yung.

When they finally reached the old Victorian house, all the lights were off. Todd unlocked the door of the apartment house, and they quietly made their way up the three flights of stairs that led to the little attic apartment.

Todd opened the apartment door, and they stepped inside. A beam of moonlight illuminated

Gin-Yung's beautiful face. He put his hand under her chin and gently tilted her face upward. Smiling, he bent his head to kiss her.

"Ahem!"

Startled, he jumped back.

A light went on and Elizabeth stood next to the bathroom in a long T-shirt, yawning. "It's about time you got here. I was getting worried."

"We were at the newspaper office," Todd said. "We found some more interesting evidence."

"Money laundering," Gin-Yung said. "Through the T. Clay Santos Construction Company."

"Then tomorrow morning, we call the federal authorities," Elizabeth said.

"Unfortunately our evidence is not only circumstantial, it's in a million pieces. Santos's thugs showed up at the office. We got out just in time."

"Doesn't matter," Elizabeth said with a smile. "Daryl Cartright wants to make a statement. But he wants to talk to Craig Maser first."

Jessica stroked Louis's forehead, watching the sun begin to rise from behind the red-and-ocher-colored mountains. They were parked on the shoulder of a rural blacktop. Finally, after hours and hours of hurtling along winding roads, they had pulled over. Louis had laid his head in Jessica's lap and fallen instantly asleep.

She looked down at him, moved by the nobility in his face. No man deserved the life he had led. No man deserved the kind of living hell Chloe had made for him. A burning hatred of Chloe rose in her breast. Jessica knew she should pity her, but she couldn't. How could she pity someone who was determined to destroy her?

Louis's gold-tipped eyelashes fluttered and he looked up at her. "Have you been watching me sleep all this time?" he asked.

She trailed her fingertips along his brow, smoothing out the frown line that seemed to have permanently creased it. "Yes. I was watching over you."

"I'm supposed to be protecting you," he said in an abashed voice, sitting up and stretching.

The sunrise lit the mountains in the distance with an orange glow. "That's where we're going," he said, gesturing toward the highest point.

"And when we get there, then what?" Jessica felt road weary in a way she never would have thought possible. All she wanted now was to stop. Even asleep in the car, the roar of the engine and the constant sound of the wheels made her feel as if she were reaching the limits of her physical endurance.

Louis clasped his hands together and brought them to his lips. "I wish I could say that our journey was over." He shook his head slowly. "But I never know what lies ahead. Or what's coming from behind." He reached into the glove compartment and pulled out a map of the United States. He unfolded it, studying the fifty states. Jessica noticed there were highlighted lines crisscrossing the country.

"What are those?" She leaned closer, looking at the map.

"That's the story of my life for the last few years. That's everywhere I've been. Everywhere I've tried to start a life. Everywhere she's found me, and turned my life into a shambles."

Jessica felt tears in her eyes. It wasn't fair. It wasn't fair that this good man should have to spend his life in fear of someone so evil. "Louis," she choked, reaching for him.

He leaned against her, and she pressed her body against his as hard as she possibly could. She wanted to make up for all the disappointment, the loss, the unhappiness he had gone through. She wished their story *were* part of a book. She wished she knew there was a happy ending for them. But she didn't.

Chapter Twelve

"*One* . . . two . . . three . . . four. *Hup* . . . two . . . three . . . four. *March* . . . two . . . three . . . four. Company! Halt!" Denise shouted.

Winston stopped, stomping one foot the way he had been taught. "Denise! There is no company here. OK? It's just me. And I'm not deaf. So you don't have to shout."

"Attention!" she thundered.

Winston rolled his eyes and shook his head. He couldn't believe Denise was actually putting them both through this farce. "Egbert!" she shouted ominously.

Sighing, Winston straightened up and stared straight ahead while Denise circled him, eyeing him from head to toe. "I'm supposed to whip you into shape. And I'm going to do it," she said in a determined voice.

"I've given this a lot of thought, and I've

decided I would rather be court-marshaled."

Denise stood on her tiptoes and shoved her heart-shaped face into his. "Winston," she said in a low, hissing tone. "You're skating on very thin ice."

"Quit threatening me," he said. "What are you trying to prove, anyway? That you're a better soldier? Well, fine. You've proved it." He threw his gun toward her, and she caught it. "You're a better man than I am, Waters. Congratulations and so long."

He pushed angrily past her and began stomping toward campus. He'd had enough of ROTC. If they wanted to throw him out of school, that was fine. He didn't care about anything anymore—except maybe salvaging whatever was left of his masculine ego after Denise had walked all over it with her combat boots.

"Winston, come back," she yelled in angry, tearful frustration. "If you want me to treat you like a man, then *be* a man. Keep your promise. Do your duty."

Winston ground his teeth. As stupid as her words sounded, she was right. He'd messed up big time. He'd been given a second chance on the condition that he join the ROTC. Walking away from that commitment was a breach of faith on his part. He might not be GI Joe by nature. But he also wasn't a cheater. He wasn't a quitter. He stopped and turned. "So what do you want me to do?" he asked.

"I want you to drop down and give me twenty," she said in a hard voice.

Winston sighed again, then dropped down to comply, positioning himself for push-ups. He hated push-ups. He hated push-ups almost more than he hated Lieutenant Drake, who was crossing the field right now, looking like Hitler might have looked if he had been from California.

"Waters!" he said in a hearty voice. "I see you're making some progress with Egbert!"

"Yes, sir," she said. "I think he's going to turn into a very good soldier if we can get a few attitude problems straightened out."

Drake smiled. "Great. Would you excuse us for a minute? Sometimes a little man-to-man talk can motivate a reluctant recruit. Build his confidence."

"Certainly." Denise executed a crisp salute and marched several steps away.

Lieutenant Drake bent down until he was facing Winston. "Egbert! Get this straight. You screw up the inspection, you screw up my life. You screw up my life, I screw up your face. Are you reading me?"

"Are you threatening me?"

"Yes," Lieutenant Drake said simply. He straightened up and smiled broadly at Denise. She came marching back. "Keep up the good work, Waters."

"Yes, sir."

"And by the way, there's an ROTC dinner tonight at the country club. Would you by any chance care to accompany me?"

Denise threw Winston a smoldering look. "Yes, sir. I'd love to, sir."

Lieutenant Drake nodded to Denise. He nodded to Winston, then he strutted off.

Winston scrambled to his feet. "You're not really going to go out with that jack-booted fascist?"

"Egbert!" she thundered. "Assume the position! And that's *an order*."

This time, Winston realized, he didn't feel like laughing. He didn't even feel like crying. What he felt like doing was kicking Commandant Waters right in the tail.

Bruce padded around the kitchen of his parents' house in his thick socks and sweatpants. His mom and dad were at work, and he had the whole house to himself.

The mansion was clean, safe, and best of all, it was quiet. He couldn't believe how much he appreciated not hearing the sound of Lila's voice. He'd never realized before how talkative she was. Talk talk talk talk. Yak yak yak yak. Before they had moved in together, he'd always considered her vivacious. Now she just seemed like sort of a motormouth.

He took a can of juice from the refrigerator and opened it. The kitchen was nice and big and fully stocked with cereal, eggs, pastries, yogurt, and snack foods of every variety. Furthermore, he could turn on the oven without worrying that it was going to blow him up.

The big color TV in the family room beckoned, and Bruce made himself comfortable on the beige suede sectional couch. He thoroughly enjoyed lying down on something that didn't raise a cloud of dust.

The phone rang. Reluctantly he picked up the receiver.

"Bruce?"

His heart sank. Lila! He guessed she'd already had a fight with her folks. She probably wanted him to come get her right now and take her back to school.

"Listen," she began in a tentative voice. "Would you mind if we didn't go back today?"

He sat up a little straighter. "No. No. I wouldn't mind at all."

"It's not that I don't want to be with you or anything, but, well . . . I thought it would be nice to spend a little time with my parents. Daddy wants to go over some business stuff and . . ."

"That's fine," he said in an eager tone. Maybe too eager. "I mean . . . that's fine." He dropped the enthusiasm level. "I'll miss you tonight, but we'll go back tomorrow."

There was a long pause.

"I was thinking maybe we could stay a couple of days," she said. "Maybe you could go see your uncle Dan and talk to him about your trust fund situation."

Bruce rolled his eyes. He really didn't appreciate Lila telling him how to run his personal business.

Uncle Dan wasn't going to budge at this point. And Bruce had no intention of making a bad situation worse by provoking the old man. But there was no sense explaining his uncle to Lila. "Yeah," he said in a noncommittal voice. "If I have time, I will."

"What else do you have to do?" she asked tartly.

Bruce took a deep breath and sat up. "Listen, Lila. I've got stuff to do. Am I supposed to give you an itinerary every morning or what?"

"Don't get mad at me. I'm just trying to help you." Her voice was low and pouty.

"Sounds to me like you're trying to run my life."

"*Your* life? I thought we were at the point where we were talking about *our* life."

Bruce scowled at the wall. "OK," he said grudgingly. "I'll call him. Happy?"

"Don't wimp out," she said curtly. And with that, she hung up.

Bruce leaned back on the sofa, crossed his feet, and reached for the TV remote control. He turned on a popular morning talk show and wondered whether or not Lila Fowler planned to make a career out of nagging him.

Tom followed Christine Benson, Glenn Fosse, and the rest of the UBC conference attendees into the enormous ballroom of the Uptown Las Vegas Hotel. The ballroom was the size of a football field. A wrestling ring had been constructed in the center, and bleachers had been installed on three sides.

The fourth wall was lined with broadcast equipment. There were large electronic decks full of switches and television monitors. A huge tech crew was busily setting up, positioning cameras and testing the sound equipment. All the men and women on the tech crew wore black bomber jackets with "UBC" emblazoned across the back.

A young UBC executive named Dave, who was in charge of organizing the events for the student broadcasters, was walking them around the area. He pointed out the technical features, talked to them about the various production problems the event represented, and described how they had arrived at the solutions to those difficulties. "OK," he said with a smile, winding up the tour. "Let's tape some drop-ins to use between the commercials. Christine, why don't we start with you?"

He handed her some copy, which she read over. Then she gave him a brisk nod. "Looks good. Where do you want to do it?"

Dave led the group over to a corner of the ballroom that had been partitioned off to use as a set. Two high stools sat in front of a large, false blue wall.

Dave indicated that she should sit down on one of the stools and signaled to a cameraman, who scurried in their direction. "Take it slow," Dave instructed. "And relax your shoulders a little more."

Tom watched Christine roll her head around on her neck, loosening the muscles so that her head would look relaxed and natural in an above-the-shoulders shot. Her short blond hair, red blazer, and white blouse looked very professional against the blue backdrop.

Dave smiled. "Good. Now get ready and . . . go."

Christine smiled, turning on her broadcast personality like a lightbulb. "Hi! I'm Christine Mulroney from Rhode Island State. There's even more excitement ahead, so stay tuned to the UBC broadcast premiere. Don't miss the match of the season between SVU's Olympic hopeful, Craig Maser, and the University of Arizona's NCAA champ, Scotty Fisher." She held the smile until the UBC director waved at her. "Cut. That was great, Christine."

"Very professional," Tom said as she hopped off the stool and came over to join him.

"Thanks," Christine answered. "I was nervous, though."

Dave clapped his hands for attention, and the group of student broadcasters fell silent. "OK. Just want to make sure we're all on track here. This is what's going to happen. We'll spend most of today shooting drops-ins and promos. The broadcast tomorrow will start with a lot of prematch programming. That's where we'll use most of the promos and drop-ins. Folks, we appreciate your coming, and we want you to have terrific pieces for your audition tapes when you get out of school. So we're going to work real hard on these pieces today. If we make you do something over and over, please be patient. We want this broadcast to look as professional as possible. And we want *you* to look as professional as possible."

He looked around and nodded at Tom. "Tom, I want you to work particularly hard at some practice interviewing today, because you won't be on tape—you'll be going on live with a prematch interview with Craig Maser."

Tom smiled. He wasn't usually an egomaniac, but he couldn't help feeling excited about the exposure he and the station would get as a result of this broadcast. The event—and the interview—would be seen on every subscribing college campus in the country. He hoped the turnout on the SVU campus would be good. The student tech crew had really gone to a lot of trouble to set up the activities hall so that it could accommodate a big crowd. Tom thought the wrestling match would probably generate a lot of interest. Craig Maser was a popular guy. And his dad was a high-profile lawyer who was currently running for Congress. Craig and his dad had been written up in several major newsmagazines.

A little flutter of excitement tickled him behind the ribs. If there was enough national interest, his interview with Maser might get picked up by the national news media. And that level of exposure might just mean a job when he got out of college.

"Tom!" Christine Mulroney elbowed him in the ribs. "Are you awake?"

Tom grinned. "Sort of."

"I tried to find that guy we ran into the other night, Paul Klaus. He said he'd help us set up some celebrity interviews. But I couldn't find him. And I can't find anybody who's heard of him."

Tom frowned, remembering the night he and Christine had come into the ballroom on their own to take a look around. A big thug had walked in and tried to throw them out. He and Tom had almost come to blows.

The scene had been interrupted by a man who called himself Paul Klaus. He had been vague about whom he worked for, but he'd seemed to have some authority, explaining that the guy who had threatened them was a freelance security man.

Klaus had been cordial in a fast-talking, superficial Las Vegas way. And when Tom and Christine had introduced themselves, he had seemed to recognize Tom's name. "We've heard about you," he had said.

Tom still wondered who he meant by "we."

"Everybody take five," the UBC executive announced. "Then we'll start shooting again. And by the way, if you made plans for tonight, cancel them. We'll be working late, and then everybody needs to get a good night's sleep."

Fat chance, Tom thought, his good spirits sinking. If he didn't get ahold of Elizabeth today, he wasn't going to sleep a wink tonight.

Chapter Thirteen

"Does Tom have any idea where you are?" Todd asked Elizabeth in a low voice late that afternoon.

They were in the kitchen making a pot of coffee. Daryl sat on the sofa in the living room of his house, waiting and fidgeting.

"I haven't called Tom. But I will," Elizabeth promised reluctantly. She'd run counter to Tom's instructions from the very beginning.

Todd knew she was putting off calling him because she was probably in for a blistering scold.

"I want to wait, though, until Daryl makes a statement," she continued. "After that, Tom can't tell me we're crazy or paranoid or anything else."

"We'll be a lot safer, too," Todd commented. He looked at his watch. Gin-Yung had left to pick up Craig Maser an hour ago.

"I don't think this is a good idea, Daryl talking to Maser."

Elizabeth shrugged. "There's nothing we can do. This was the condition Daryl set. I think he feels that if he can save somebody else's career, it'll make losing his own easier to live with." She sighed unhappily. "I wish we knew whether we were ultimately helping Daryl or hurting him."

Todd poured the hot coffee into mugs. "We talked about this before. Those guys are exploiting athletes and ruining people's lives. Daryl's in for some rough treatment, but we're going to stick by him. And we'll do whatever we can to help him. At least I will." He put his arm around Elizabeth and gave her a grateful hug. "I've been a down-and-out athlete myself. I know how much it means to have friends who help and support you."

Elizabeth smiled and got the milk out of the refrigerator. "Think we can trust Maser?"

Todd shrugged. "He obviously didn't like Mark Gathers, which tells me he doesn't like the choices he's making about his career. Can we trust him not to report back to Santos? That I don't know."

The door opened with a bang, and Todd and Elizabeth both jumped nervously. Todd stuck his head out of the kitchen and smiled. It was Gin-Yung—and she had Craig Maser with her.

Todd felt a surge of pride in his girlfriend. Everybody in the sports department knew Gin-Yung. And almost everybody liked her. She was an honest reporter who loved sports and admired athletes. They trusted her. Only Gin-Yung could

151

have gotten a star athlete to come to Daryl's run-down neighborhood for reasons unknown the day before the biggest match of his career.

Craig started a bit when he saw Todd and Elizabeth. "What's going on?"

Gin-Yung put a small hand on Craig's large arm. "It's cool. Don't worry. We're all friends here."

Craig's eyes darted around and rested on Daryl. Daryl stood slowly. "Hey, Craig. Remember me?"

"Sure," Craig said after a moment. He stepped forward and clasped Daryl's hand. "You were a star basketball player last year. I remember you very well."

Daryl's lips turned up, but it was a sad smile. "Yeah. Well, a lot of people have forgotten me. And they'll forget you too, Craig."

Craig looked warily from face to face. "What are you talking about?"

"You know what I'm talking about," Daryl said. "And starting tomorrow, everybody else is going to know too."

"I haven't done anything wrong," Craig said.

"You're supposed to take a dive tomorrow, aren't you?" Todd asked.

Craig's face flushed. "Why am I here? What do you want?"

"Look, I got paid to shave points. Fumble the ball. They convinced me to blow my career and disappear," Daryl said. "I thought I was making the right choice at the time. But I'm telling you now, I regret the decision. So don't make the same mistake I did."

Craig looked almost sick.

"Gamblers have infiltrated the whole athletics department. And tomorrow I'm going to make a statement to the public and to the federal authorities that's going to bust these guys' operation right out of the water. I just wanted to warn you, before it's too late. Don't take that dive tomorrow. Stay clean and you'll still have a career."

Craig looked stricken. "I don't know what to do," he whispered, almost to himself.

"When do you leave for Las Vegas?" Daryl asked.

"Tonight," Craig said. "Mark Gathers is supposed to pick me up and take me to the airport."

"Are you going to tell Mark what we talked about here?" Todd asked bluntly.

Craig lifted his chin. "No."

"Come on," Gin-Yung said, pulling at Craig's sleeve. "I'll take you back to your dorm."

"Don't forget what I said," Daryl said. "Once I make my statement, they're going to be taking a close look at everybody in the athletics department. Make sure you don't have anything to hide."

"Would you like another soda?" Thomas Drake asked Denise.

"Thank you," she said, feeling a little shy. The officers' dance at the country club was a very formal occasion. She was wearing a dress uniform that made her fit right in, but she wasn't used to so much ceremony. Still, she couldn't help feeling proud to be here with Lieutenant Thomas Drake. ROTC personnel from all over California had come to Sweet Valley for the dinner, including a lot of top-ranking officers and several soldiers from her own unit.

When he was screaming on the field with the cords of his neck standing out, she hadn't realized how handsome Lieutenant Drake really was. Right now, the classic features of his bronzed face made him look like a matinee idol from a forties movie about World War II. Not only was he tall, with broad shoulders, a narrow waist, and slim hips, he also carried himself with an air of assurance that was refreshing after Winston's slouching diffidence.

Denise felt her heart flutter guiltily. She set her small jaw and hardened her heart. Winston was a slacker and a cheater, she reminded herself. Sure, he felt bad about having cheated—but only because the act had made her mad and gotten him into trouble. He didn't have any real character. No real backbone. No spine.

"So, Private Waters," an older man with a lot of medals said. "How long have you been a member of the ROTC?"

"Only a few days, sir," she answered.

He smiled. "How do you like it so far?"

"So far, she's been an excellent recruit," Lieutenant Drake answered, handing her a glass of soda.

154

"Excellent," the older man commented enthusiastically before disappearing into the throng.

"Hey, Drake," another guy said, coming up to join them with a group of uniformed friends. "I hear your qualifying inspection is day after tomorrow."

"That's right," Lieutenant Drake answered.

"Worried?"

"Not really," he replied in a smug voice, putting his arm around Denise. "I've got a good outfit. An outstanding group of men and women. I have every confidence that they will be a credit to the ROTC program and to me."

"What about that big goofball we keep hearing about?" the guy asked. "Egbert."

There was a burst of raucous laughter from his friends.

"Egbert," someone else repeated in a voice of incredulous contempt. "What kind of name is that, anyway?"

"A goofball name," somebody answered, drawing hoots of laughter from the group.

"The guy can't take two steps without falling over his own feet," someone else commented.

"He's an embarrassment."

"He's a loser."

"He's a wimp."

Denise felt almost physically ill as she waited for Lieutenant Drake to put a stop to this cruel and childish ridicule. Thomas was a mature leader type. She was pretty disgusted with Winston herself, but that didn't mean she wanted to hear the man with whom she had been in love for the last several months be totally trashed.

"Yeah, Drake. What are you going to do about that bum?" a redheaded guy with a crew cut asked.

Denise waited for Lieutenant Drake to reprimand the group for their harsh criticism of a comrade-in-arms.

But Drake said nothing, and his lips curved into a contemptuous smile. "Is that guy the ultimate weirdo misfit or what? Denise here really deserves a medal. She worked with him for two hours today."

Hot tears welled up in Denise's eyes. She felt sorry for Winston. Although she still felt angry with him for having such a bad attitude, she was ashamed of herself for not standing up for him. But most of all, she felt incredibly disillusioned with Lieutenant Drake.

A real leader stood up for his men and women. A mature man didn't call people names or make fun of them because they were different.

She took a sip of her soda, and her hand shook with anger. Drake didn't look like a war hero anymore. He just looked like an overgrown Boy Scout. And a bully.

"So are you nervous or what?"

Craig didn't answer, and Mark's hands tightened on the wheel. He couldn't really blame him for being distracted and uncommunicative. The guy's career was going down the toilet tomorrow.

Mark wondered what Santos offered him. He would have asked the guy if he didn't think Maser would bust him in the chops for asking.

The airport lights blinked up ahead. Mark signaled and turned off, heading toward the far terminal. "Las Vegas is supposed to be a fun town," Mark said, making one last attempt to draw Craig out. Still Craig didn't answer.

When Coach Crane had told Mark to drive Craig to the airport, Mark wondered if it was going to be an uncomfortable drive. Craig didn't like him—and he hadn't tried to keep his feelings a secret.

But Craig had seemed preoccupied ever since they left the SVU campus. Mark had actually made one or two baiting remarks, but Craig had ignored them. Clearly Craig Maser had only one thing on his mind—the match tomorrow.

Tomorrow was going to be an eventful day, Mark thought with a flicker of fear. He just hoped it wasn't *too* eventful.

Love hurts was the repeating refrain of one of Jessica's favorite songs. The radio flickered in and out, and it seemed to Jessica that every time the sound flickered in, the same song was playing.

Before Jessica and Louis had fallen in love, when they were first becoming friends, Jessica had had a series of bad relationships. At eighteen, she fiercely insisted that she no longer subscribed to the myth of romantic love or the dependability of men. Louis had gently laughed at her youthful cynicism. *"Chivalry is not dead,"* he had jokingly informed her.

Love hurts, she had quoted in a cynical comeback, making him laugh.

At the time, neither one of them had any way of knowing how prophetic that particular exchange would turn out to be. Jessica snapped off the radio. She didn't want to hear that song again. "Louis," she said, pulling over to the sidewalk of a small town in the mountains. "We've got to stop. I can't keep going. I just can't."

Louis lifted his head from the seat back and gazed sleepily around. "Where are we?"

"I have no idea," Jessica said. She had been driving for the past several hours while Louis slept fitfully. Now she too was exhausted and almost hallucinating with fatigue. She turned off the engine.

The sudden quiet was a relief. Jessica rolled down the window, letting the cool mountain air refresh her. "I wonder how Elizabeth is doing."

Louis lifted his hand and caressed her cheek. "Do you miss her?"

"Yes and no." Jessica smiled sadly. "Elizabeth always makes things come out all right. She'll get this thing solved, and then we'll go back. We'll figure out what to do about Chloe. There are laws now about stalking and . . ."

Louis hung his head.

"We *will* go back," Jessica said. "I've been thinking about this all day. We can't run forever."

Louis rubbed his eyes. "Jessica, I don't ever want to lie to you. You're right. We can't run forever. But we can't hide from the future forever, either. When it's safe for you to go back, you're going to go back. But I can't. I've got no job. I can't even look for another job with this mess on my record. Basically, I can't give you any kind of life at all."

"I won't go back without you," she said vehemently.

"Yes, you will," he said. "The only reason I brought you with me was to keep you from getting hurt. But we can only stay ahead of Chloe for so long. She'll find me. She always does. And when she zeros in, anybody around me is in danger. I won't take that chance with you."

"It's not *your* choice anymore," Jessica said, speaking angrily to him for the first time in their relationship. "Look. I'm slowly but surely developing a mind of my own. I'm in love with you. I will always be in love with you. As far as I'm concerned, we have no choice. We have to be together."

Louis ran his hands through his hair. "Let's not talk about this right now. We're both too exhausted to be reasonable."

Jessica's jaw muscles tensed, and she stared out the window. She didn't care how tired she was or wasn't. She knew she wasn't going to change her mind.

Louis reached over and put his hand gently on her neck, moving it in slow circles to relax her. "The road does this to you after a while," he said. "It creates a sense of . . . unending despair. I understand how you feel. We'll stop," he promised. "We'll find a place to stay. Someplace private. We both need to rest."

Her spine relaxed, and she gave him a tight smile. She wasn't going to change her mind. But there was no sense in fighting about the future here and now. All she wanted at the moment was to stop. To stop moving. To stop running. She was anxious for a respite from the constant noise of the car and the road.

"Look at that," Louis said, pointing to a quaint house on the side of the road. Above a red front door was a sign that announced that the place was a real estate office. "Maybe we should see if they've got something we can rent."

"It's late. I'm sure they're closed."

"We'll try anyway," Louis insisted. "The porch light is on. Whoever runs the office probably lives there. Let's knock and see what happens."

They got out of the car and walked up to the door. Louis rang the bell.

After a long moment a light went on inside, and the door opened a crack. An older lady peered out. "Can I help you?"

"Hi. I know it's late. But we were looking for a

place to spend a couple of nights," Louis said. "We've been traveling for a while and . . ."

"You'd like to rest your weary bones," the woman finished for him, opening the door wider.

Louis's green eyes were sunken with fatigue. But they still glowed when he smiled. Jessica could tell the real estate lady was responding to his warm charm. "Yes," he said. "We thought we could keep driving, but we're both so tired, we're probably not safe behind the wheel."

The lady opened the door and invited them into the front room, which was obviously her office. "There's a motel ten miles down the highway," she said. "If you're just looking for a place to spend a night or two, that's probably your best bet. I don't rent properties by the night."

Louis shrugged. "We'd like someplace private if possible. And quiet. Something off the main road. We could take it for longer than a couple of nights. We're traveling cross-country, pretty much following our noses. And frankly, we've had enough of impersonal motels. We'd like something that feels a little more personal."

She smiled and winked. "Newlyweds, eh? My husband and I had the same kind of honeymoon. But we drove a camper."

He laughed gently. "Maybe we'll do that on our second honeymoon."

Jessica smiled. Louis wasn't a very good liar. But they probably *looked* so much like they belonged together that the woman believed him. She knew Louis didn't have any intention of staying a week. But they didn't want to get a room in a motel on the highway where they might be seen.

The woman pulled a small map out from underneath the counter. "I've got a little guest farm for rent about six miles up that way. Two stories. Furnished. A barn in the back. I can let you have it for a week. Will that do?"

Louis nodded and bent over the map. "That will be fine," he said. "Just show me how to get there."

Tom's feet made no noise on the thickly carpeted hallway of the hotel. He put the key in the lock of his door and cried out in alarm. The door had suddenly swung open, and two men came out and grabbed him by the lapels. Quickly they pulled him into the room and threw him up against the wall.

One of the men was Max, the guy who had tried to eject Tom from the ballroom. Tom didn't recognize the other attacker. But he had *thug* written all over him.

"We've got a message for you," Max said, pushing his acne-scarred face close to Tom's. "Tell your girlfriend to back off. Or somebody's going to get hurt."

"What are you talking about?" Tom shouted.

"I'm talking about Daryl Cartright."

"Who?" Tom clenched his teeth and stared Max straight in the eye.

"If Daryl causes any problems, some little people are going to get hurt."

"What are you talking about?" Tom demanded again.

The man shoved Tom against the wall. "Just tell her," he said. He released his grip on Tom, and the two men left the room, closing the door behind them.

Tom ran his hand over his hair, feeling the sore spot that was already forming on the back of his head where it had hit the wall. He reached for the phone and dialed Elizabeth's number. The phone rang and rang. Still no answer. Still no machine.

He tried Gin-Yung's room. Her machine was on. "It's Tom. Please call me in Vegas as soon as you get this. Something's up." He could hear the tremor in his voice, and he hoped that Gin-Yung didn't freak out when she got the message. "If I'm not in my room, have the switchboard page me," he added, before hanging up the phone.

He dialed Todd. There was no answer, and Todd didn't seem to have an answering machine.

He called the station. No answer. Just a recording.

He picked up the phone and threw it across the room. It landed with a loud, but unsatisfying, crash.

"This place is beautiful," Jessica said happily.

The farmhouse was high in the mountains and set two miles back from the road. They had stopped at the local grocery and stocked up on food and drinks before winding their way up the road to the remote farmhouse. The house was so far in the mountains that there was no phone or television or radio. They were as isolated as it was possible for two people to be.

They had explored the land around the house briefly, but it was too dark to see much. The house itself was small, but it had two floors. Upstairs was a large bedroom with a four-poster bed and a large, hand-painted wardrobe. There was also a large bathroom with a tub, in which Jessica and Louis had enjoyed a long, relaxing soak.

After they had bathed, they gorged themselves on steak and green salad. On the ground floor was a kitchen with a gas stove, an old refrigerator, and a wooden table with wooden chairs. Cheerful curtains made of red bandanna material hung from the windows, and the same fabric covered the cushions of the chairs.

There was a small parlor that was filled with funny, faux Victorian furniture. Louis had laughed and commented, "Early funeral home." But the living room was cozy and welcoming. The sofa was old but soft, covered with tan corduroy. A red, blue, and pink afghan hung over the back of it. There were two platform rockers and the bookshelves were lined with old volumes that emanated a dusty smell—which Louis considered the most intoxicating perfume in the world.

He had pulled down several volumes and now

sat flipping through a book of love poems while Jessica lay across the sofa with her head on his knee.

"How about this one? Do you remember this?" He began to read a poem. They had studied the piece, by Longfellow, in his class. The words told the story of a Viking who fled with his stolen love to the new world. There he built her a tower over which his spirit stood guard for centuries.

The sentiment was old-fashioned and corny, but Jessica loved the poem because it was romantic. When Louis finished reading, she yawned and stretched. "I love that poem. I can see you in armor, guarding me in a tower."

He smiled. "Are you ready to return to your tower?"

In answer, she lifted her arms and put them around his neck. He picked her up, carrying her easily upstairs to the bedroom.

Chapter
Fourteen

"Did you call him?" Lila asked as soon as Bruce picked up the phone.

"Lila." He sighed heavily. "I just don't think you understand . . ."

Lila stretched out on her luxurious bed and listened while Bruce went into some totally lame excuse about why he wasn't going to argue with his uncle Dan.

She slumped down, resting her head on one of the many oversize feather pillows that were stacked against the quilted headboard of her expensive antique bed.

Her parents had been delighted to see her, and Mrs. Fowler had suggested a shopping trip this afternoon. Lila had readily agreed. Her mother always encouraged Lila to charge whatever she wanted to her father's credit card.

So far, she hadn't told her parents that she was

broke and living with Bruce. They were so busy fawning over her and spoiling her, she hated to ruin things.

Besides, she was relieved to be back in her parents' opulent home instead of in that dump with Bruce. As she listened to Bruce go on and on about his uncle, he sounded wimpier and wimpier. Now that she'd had some time to herself, she wasn't sure she and Bruce could even be happy together in a place like Fowler Crest. She had missed him a little last night, but hearing his voice and his excuses was making her remember what an irritating personality he had sometimes.

"Never mind," she finally snapped. "It doesn't matter."

"Why don't you call me when you're ready to go back," Bruce suggested.

"OK," Lila agreed. She hung up the phone with a sigh, realizing that she might *never* be ready to go back to a life with Bruce.

"Where are you?" Jessica cried. "Louis? Where are you?"

Louis saw her feet emerging through the tall wildflowers and leapt up. She giggled as he pulled her down on top of him. Still laughing, they rolled over and over in the field of buttercups.

"What's so funny?" he asked after she'd struggled to sit up.

Jessica shrugged and brushed a fleck of yellow powder off the end of his nose. She held it up for him to inspect. In response, he took his finger and wiped the buttercup dust off the end of *her* nose. "There's a lot of that going around."

Jessica laughed and fell forward on her stomach, smelling the grass and the wildflowers and the fresh, sharp air. Insects buzzed loudly in the warm grass. "I never thought of myself as the outdoor type," she joked. "But I could spend the rest of my life on this land."

Louis rolled over on his back and put an arm behind his head. "So could I. We've got each other. We've got books. We've got food. We've got a fireplace."

"So why not stay put?" she said.

A dark cloud seemed to descend over his face.

"She won't find us," Jessica insisted. "Louis, I twisted and turned and twisted and turned until even *I* didn't know what road I was on."

He groaned. "That sounds like a metaphor for my life," he said wryly.

"Everything's going to work out," she said, feeling more positive about the future now that they were *settled* somewhere. "And you'll teach again. I just know it."

He smiled as if he didn't believe her but was prepared to play along. "Of course I will."

"If you didn't teach, what would you want to do?" she asked curiously.

His lips curved inward and disappeared while he contemplated the question. "There isn't anything," he said finally. "I've never wanted to do anything else. My father was a teacher. And he always maintained that teaching was the noblest profession." Louis smiled shyly. "He was a historian too. Not a medievalist, but he was interested in the period. I used to love hearing him tell stories about Ivanhoe and King Arthur."

He blushed and turned over on his side, propping his head up on his elbow. "When I was about ten years old, I fell out of a tree. I was pretty badly injured. And my dad was told that I might not walk again. By that age, my dad and I were alone. My mom died when I was very young."

"I didn't know that," Jessica said softly. She was instantly filled with sadness at the thought of Louis without a mother.

"We haven't known each other that long," he reminded her.

"That's true," she conceded. "But go on with the story. What happened?"

Louis pulled a flower from the ground and arranged it behind Jessica's ear as he spoke. "That was a hard year for me. Looking back, I realize it must have been even harder for my dad. But when you're a child, you don't see things like that. I just saw myself as a prisoner in my room—subjected to all kinds of torturous therapies and exercises and medicines. My only escape was books. I read stories about knights, codes of honor, and selfless deeds performed for beautiful women. I remember thinking, if a man can fight a dragon or rescue a maiden from an enemy army, then I can overcome this injury."

When the flower was arranged to his satisfaction, Louis drew back his head and admired his work. "The healing process took two years. But eventually I learned to walk again. I went back to school, and my life went on. But I had made a decision that when I grew up, I was going to do noble things. As I got older, I realized that I would never fight a dragon. I would never rescue a maiden. But I had seen my father give of himself year after year to his students, often with very little reward. That, to me, seemed to be a noble thing. So I chose to become a teacher."

Louis sat up and tugged at his ear. "Instead, I wound up ruining the life of a beautiful young woman and running away from my dragon. When you get right down to it, I'm sort of a failure as a knight."

"Not to me," Jessica said quietly. She lay on her back and pulled him close.

Tom took his place on one of the stools that had been acquired for his live interview with Craig Maser. Beside him Craig sat in his wrestling shorts and a bright yellow robe. UBC was about to go on air, and the ballroom was filling rapidly.

Nearby a cameraman carefully positioned his equipment. Across the room the large UBC tech crew tested sound, lights, and transmission gear. All nine TV monitors were turned on and tuned to the local cable news channel that would make way for the UBC broadcast when it began.

Tom straightened his tie, noticing that Craig seemed nervous and fidgety. Then again, Tom himself felt pretty nervous and fidgety. In addition to his fears about being on live television, he was still shaken up over the obtuse warning he'd received the night before. The cameraman said something about replacing a lens and disappeared.

Craig gave Tom a tight smile. "This is some big deal, huh?"

Tom looked at the wrestler a long time, then tried a shot in the dark. "Do you know Daryl Cartright?"

Craig's face turned pale. "Why do you want to know?"

Tom bit his lip. "I got an unusual message delivered to me last night."

"Hey, Tom!" a techie called from the deck of monitors. "Come over here. Sweet Valley University is on the news."

Tom jumped off his stool and ran over to the monitors. Craig was right behind him. Every monitor showed the same visual image. On the screens was an establishing shot of SVU's large athletics complex. The picture was followed by another shot of the student union. Then the camera swung around and closed in on several men in suits, who were climbing out of a black car and walking purposely toward the front steps. They wore sunglasses and looked like FBI types.

A sound engineer removed his headphones and flipped a switch so that they could listen to the voice-over. "Federal marshals have been asked to investigate a scandal in the SVU athletics department," announced a deep-voiced newscaster. "According to an anonymous tip, student reporters have allegedly stumbled onto a five-year point-shaving and money-laundering scheme involving not only former athletes but also administration officials. And they say they *do* have a witness."

The camera showed a picture of Dr. Beal and Coach Crane walking to the student union building.

"Administration officials maintain that the allegations are fallacious and have called a press conference to deny the accusations. They say the rumor is an attempt to sabotage their growing athletics program."

"Holy-moly." Christine whistled, appearing behind Tom. "Did you guys know anything about this?"

Tom's heart was beating like a timpani drum inside his chest. He was so furious he thought he might explode. "Excuse me," he said, breaking away from the group and tearing out of the ballroom.

He careened into the lobby, running toward the elevator. He wanted to get to his room—and to a telephone.

Elizabeth was crazy, and so was Todd Wilkins. How dare they go off like a couple of loose cannons and call in federal marshals? Did they have any idea how stupid they were going to look if they couldn't prove their allegations?

And if their allegations *were* true, did they have any idea how much danger they were in?

Last night, he had merely worried that Elizabeth and Todd were rekindling their romance. Now he was worried that something might have happened to her. No wonder he'd been accosted last night. Obviously someone knew that he was involved with Elizabeth.

"Tom Watts! Is there a Tom Watts in the room? I have an emergency page for Tom Watts."

Tom skidded to a stop and saw a bellhop walking through the lobby, holding a mobile phone. "Here!" Tom shouted. "I'm Tom Watts." The bellboy walked briskly toward Tom and handed him the phone. "You can return it to the desk when you're finished," he said, retreating to give Tom some privacy.

"Hello! Hello!" Tom shouted into the telephone.

"Tom?"

He could barely hear her voice over the noise in the background. "Tom. It's me, Elizabeth."

"Where are you? Are you OK?" He put a hand over one ear to try to block out the noise in the lobby.

"I'm fine," her voice crackled. "At least I am for now."

Tom stepped around the corner into a quiet hallway where he could speak without being overheard. "This connection is terrible," he said, trying to project his voice over the static.

"I'm calling from a cellular phone," she said. "Got a pencil? Here's the number."

Tom pulled a pencil and pad from his jacket and quickly jotted down the number. "OK. Now. You want to fill me in *before* I lose my temper and scream—or *after*?"

He heard her chuckle at the other end of the connection. "I'm in the student activities hall. Tom, the place is a zoo."

The student activities hall looked like the pictures of Mardi Gras that Elizabeth had seen on the news. The room was filled wall to wall with students. Many of them had gathered to watch the Maser-Fisher match and witness the debut of the UBC satellite channel.

Others had heard or seen the news about the press conference and had surged toward the building, eager to hear what Dr. Beal and Coach Crane had to say about the alleged point-shaving scandal. The news media were everywhere. Trucks from all the major networks were parked outside, and reporters circulated through the crowded room, interviewing students and looking for information.

Daryl hadn't arrived yet. Gin-Yung had picked him up not too long ago. Now she was waiting at Lila and Bruce's for the signal to bring him to the campus.

"Elizabeth!" she heard Tom shout on the other end of the line. "I got a message."

"I didn't leave any message," she said.

She could hear Tom saying something through the static about somebody getting hurt. But between the roar of the crowd and the static on the line, his words were impossible to make out.

Elizabeth pressed her ear closer to the phone. "Tom. This is important, so listen. As soon as Daryl makes a statement, we'll all be safe," she shouted. "Santos and the gamblers won't be able to do anything once Daryl tells what he knows. Tom! Craig Maser knows what's going to happen. Tell him everything is falling into place. OK?"

Elizabeth spotted two men in suits and sunglasses. They weren't wearing badges, but she knew immediately that they were federal marshals. "I've got to go. The feds have arrived."

"Elizabeth! Elizabeth, wait!" he cried.

Elizabeth pressed the button with her thumb and then quickly dialed the number at Lila's apartment. Gin-Yung picked up the phone. "Hello?"

"Bring Daryl," Elizabeth said. "It's show time."

Chapter
Fifteen

"Thank you all for gathering here today," Coach Crane said into the microphone.

The noise in the crowded student activities hall died down as everyone waited to hear what Coach Crane had to say. The monitors mounted on the walls had not yet picked up the closed-circuit broadcast from Las Vegas, and Coach Crane's face stared out across the hall from every large screen. His voice seemed amplified to ten times its normal volume.

Todd watched the door for signs of Gin-Yung and Daryl. Across the room, Elizabeth looked tense and white.

"This large turnout is a wonderful testament to our school spirit," Coach Crane said. "We're all justifiably very proud of Craig Maser."

The crowd cheered and applauded while Coach Crane smiled broadly, acknowledging the applause on Craig's behalf. He held up his hands, signaling that he was ready to resume speaking. Aside from a low murmuring of whispers, the students became silent as they waited for him to continue.

"This broadcast is a historic event. The University Broadcasting Company is a welcome addition to campus life, and we're proud to be a part of its launch. I'm going to step aside now and let Dr. Beal speak."

Coach Crane stood back and Dr. Beal stepped forward, looking dignified and credible in a dark suit. "Thank you, Coach Crane," he said into the microphone. "I want to welcome you all and extend my personal best wishes to Mr. Maser." He smiled broadly. "I know we're all expecting him to win."

The hall erupted into cheers and whistles.

Dr. Beal lifted his hands and asked for quiet. "I applaud your enthusiasm. And I would also like to take this opportunity to thank our Alumni Association, whose generosity has underwritten the cost of this event."

He paused and smiled thinly, acknowledging the next round of applause. When it died down, his face became grave. He cleared his throat as if he now had something distasteful he was obliged to say. "It's a shame that occasions like this have to be marred by any unpleasantness, but unfortunately I have a duty to speak out today. I must refute the accusations that have irresponsibly been leveled against the administration and the athletics department of this university. These accusations are the work of a disgruntled ex-athlete and a power-hungry reporter. There is no foundation for any of their theories. Their abhorrent mudslinging is a malicious attempt to libel and defame myself, Coach Crane, and Mr. T. Clay Santos, the generous president of our SVU Alumni Association."

Gin-Yung and Daryl Cartright appeared in the doorway. A ripple of whispers filtered through the room. The crowd parted as if by a signal, and Daryl's tall frame moved easily toward the podium. He looked handsome, confident, and all-American in clean straight-legged jeans, a white oxford cloth shirt, and a green V-neck sweater.

Todd felt his nerves begin to settle a little. Daryl looked as credible as Dr. Beal. He looked like a guy whom everyone would believe.

Dr. Beal's hard eyes followed Daryl's progress. "A free press is a good thing. But when members of that press use their power to slander and libel honest, well-meaning teachers, professionals, and philanthropists, it is time to call those reporters to account for their actions. There will be consequences," he said in an ominous tone.

Daryl stood at the edge of the platform now, and Dr. Beal looked at him coldly. "Mr. Cartright. Am I right in understanding that you want to make a statement?"

"That's correct," Daryl said in a loud, clear tone. He marched quickly up the steps and walked over to the microphone. After adjusting the mike so that it was at the right level, he cleared his throat. Then he pulled a folded-up piece of paper from his pocket. "My name is Daryl Cartright," he read. "I'm a former member of the SVU basketball team. I would like to go on record today as categorically denying the allegations made by reporters from the campus TV station, WSVU. I do not know why they have said the things they have said. And I do not know why they have used my name in connection with this matter."

Todd shook his head, unable to believe what he was hearing. "I have nothing but the highest regard for Coach Crane, Dr. Beal, and the Sweet Valley University athletics system. I hope someday to be a part of it again. I also hope that there will be no more intrusions on my family life from reporters."

Elizabeth was staring at Daryl like somebody who'd been hit over the head with a hammer. Todd began shouldering his way through the crowd in her direction. Santos had gotten to Daryl. He didn't know how or when. And he didn't know what had made Daryl betray them. But there was no doubt that Todd, Elizabeth, and probably Gin-Yung were in terrible danger.

The crowd was murmuring angrily, and Todd could see a lot of resentful stares being directed at Elizabeth.

"Some people will do anything for publicity," one girl said with a sniff.

"Does being a reporter mean you have to be a

total slimeball?" somebody else commented.

"Does she hate the athletics department or what?" a big football player shouted angrily.

Todd grabbed Elizabeth's arm. "Let's get out of here."

Elizabeth started toward the podium. "Daryl!" she yelled. "What are you doing? Why are you lying?"

Her cry brought the crowd's anger to the surface.

"Leave him alone," a guy with a beard said.

Daryl slipped unobtrusively out a side door, and Todd grabbed Elizabeth. "Come on. Let's get Gin-Yung and take off."

"No." Elizabeth started forward toward the exit door.

"I want to talk to him."

Todd sighed deeply. Having no choice, he took off after her, signaling to Gin-Yung to follow. Gin-Yung's small head was visible darting through the crowd. After a minute Todd felt her fingers clutch at the back of his windbreaker.

Todd, Elizabeth, and Gin-Yung hurried out the exit door. Several yards ahead Daryl was striding across the green. "Daryl," Todd shouted. "Daryl, wait!"

Daryl wouldn't turn. When he reached the curb, a long black car pulled up beside him. Bobbo and the big guy who looked just like him jumped out of the backseat.

Elizabeth broke into a run toward the car.

"Daryl! What did they do? What did they promise you?"

Bobbo shoved Elizabeth hard on the shoulder, and she fell back against Todd. "Leave him alone," Bobbo said.

Daryl ducked into the car. Bobbo and the other guy got in behind him and slammed the door. The driver hit the gas and the long sedan drove away.

Gin-Yung pressed her head against Todd's arm and groaned. "I can't believe he did that. I picked him up at his house, drove him here, and never got any vibes at all that he was going to sell us out. I'm so sorry. I guess I'm losing my touch."

Todd put his arm around her. "It's not your fault. How could you possibly have known?"

The phone tucked in Elizabeth's jacket rang. She pulled it from her pocket. "Hello?" she said.

"Elizabeth. It's me, Tom. I'm in the hallway outside the ballroom. What's going on? I just watched the news on the monitors. Every station is showing Daryl Cartright *denying* any rumors."

"Daryl betrayed us," Elizabeth said, her voice thick with emotion. "We don't know why."

"What I was trying to tell you before was that somebody came into my room last night. They said somebody was going to get hurt—starting with the smallest. Where's Gin-Yung? Is she with you? Maybe she's in danger. Maybe Daryl was afraid she was going to get hurt."

"They didn't mean Gin-Yung," Elizabeth said

slowly, her mind putting all the pieces in place. "They meant Daryl's brothers and his sister."

"What?"

"I didn't think even Santos would resort to something so evil," Elizabeth said tearfully. "But Daryl's got a little sister and two little brothers. Santos must have threatened to hurt them if Daryl told the truth."

Todd pulled at her sleeve, and Elizabeth turned around. "Tom! Hold on."

"Tell him to tell Maser," Todd said. "Craig needs to know what's going on. We can't let him take a chance without knowing the risks."

"Elizabeth," Tom said. "We're going on live in two minutes. I've got to go. I'll call you back as soon as my interview with Craig Maser is over."

Elizabeth spoke urgently into the phone. Todd was right. Craig had a right to know just how much danger was involved in crossing T. Clay Santos. "Listen, Tom. Tell Craig Maser that Daryl didn't make a statement because Santos threatened his family. Craig needs to know that before the match, OK?"

"Are you telling me Craig Maser's involved in this?" Tom asked.

"I'm not telling you anything over a cellular phone," Elizabeth said. "But just tell him what happened. Right now we're going back into the activities hall. We'll watch the match from there. Good luck."

She turned off the phone and put it back in her

pocket. Then she, Todd, and Gin-Yung stared at each other in silence.

"What do you think Craig will do?" Gin-Yung asked finally.

Elizabeth pinched the bridge of her nose. "I don't know. If he's smart, he'll do what Santos paid him to do. The man will obviously stoop to any level to get what he wants. If Craig Maser gets hurt because of us . . ." She shook her head as her voice trailed off. "If *anybody* gets hurt because of us, I'll hang up my investigative reporter's license forever."

"Come on," Todd said, putting a comforting hand on her shoulder. "Let's go back inside. We won't be popular, but I think it's important that we stay visible. We can't look like we're caving."

Tom walked into the crowded ballroom, a technician beside him. His heart was still pounding from his conversation with Elizabeth, and the air in the crowded room was stifling.

"Here's the rundown," said the tech. "We'll do the intro. Then you'll do a short prematch interview with Craig. So why don't you get Craig and go over and sit on the stools. We'll get the camera set up."

Craig was standing by the monitors, watching the news feeds. His face was like a block of granite. Tom went over and tapped him on the shoulder. "Craig, we need to get situated for the interview."

Craig nodded but said nothing. The wrestler looked around, his eyes darting nervously from one door to the other, as if he were wishing he could make his escape.

They sat down on the stools. "I've got a message from Elizabeth Wakefield," Tom said as he clipped tiny microphones to their lapels.

Craig's face turned even paler, and Tom began to feel slightly sick to his stomach. He'd spent the whole conference worrying about his relationship with Elizabeth. But he'd stayed in Las Vegas because his being there was in the best interests of the station, the school, and his own future career. But now none of his work seemed worth the effort.

The whole process of news and sports was tainted with corruption. He couldn't accuse Craig with no evidence. He was going to have to conduct the interview as if he really believed that the match Craig was about to take part in was going to be a contest. Like it or not, Tom was an unwilling accomplice. "Elizabeth said to tell you that Daryl didn't make a statement because his little sister and brothers were threatened."

Craig rubbed his forehead with his palms, as if he were trying to make his brain work faster. He removed his hands and bit his lower lip. "Did she tell you anything about me?"

Tom shook his head. "Nope."

"This interview is going out live, right?"

Tom nodded.

"Tom! Craig!"

Both boys jumped when the UBC director and his assistants appeared The director wore headphones, aviator glasses, and a very tense expression on his face. "OK," he said in an authoritative voice, glancing at his clipboard. "You all have sixty seconds."

Chapter Sixteen

"Professor Miles?" a deep voice said.

"Yes?" Louis felt a familiar anxious sensation the minute he opened the door. The two men standing on the porch wore dark suits. They were extremely polite and very somber. Louis knew from past experience that they were police detectives.

"I'm Detective Hale, and this is Detective Farris." The man nodded toward his partner. "We got your name from Mrs. Jenkins, the proprietor of these guest farms."

"Is something wrong?" Louis asked, looking out the door and over their shoulders.

"Are you alone?" Detective Farris asked.

"No," he answered. "I'm traveling with . . . my girlfriend."

A look passed between the two detectives. Louis stiffened as he read the disapproval in their eyes.

"I'm afraid there's been an accident," Detective Hale, the older of the two, stated in a grim voice. "We found the body of a woman in a car nearby. Her identification indicates that she is Mrs. Louis Miles."

Louis felt his legs begin to buckle beneath him.

"We found her in her car. The engine was on and the windows were rolled up. The cause of death looks like carbon monoxide poisoning—self-inflicted."

"Suicide?" he whispered.

The detective nodded. Louis walked into the living room, and the two men followed. He sat down in an overstuffed chair and ran his hands through his hair, hating himself for the sense of relief he was feeling. It was over. Finally the long nightmare of his marriage was over.

"For the record, we'll need you to identify the body," Detective Farris informed him. "Could you come with us right now?"

Louis nodded. "Let me get my coat." He grabbed his jacket off the back of the sofa. No need to wake Jessica. This would only upset her.

A few moments later he was in the back of the police car, winding down the long mountain to the small area hospital. The ride took no more than five minutes. And time seemed to be passing at a surreal speed. Staring out the car window, Louis felt as if he were periodically blacking out. One minute he was in the back of the car, the next minute he was walking down the white hallway of the hospital.

He blinked against the harsh fluorescent lights overhead. An air conditioner seemed to be going full blast, causing Louis to shiver. He followed the detectives until they reached a room marked MORGUE.

"This way." Detective Hale opened the door and stepped back so Louis could enter. The room was covered with white tile and stainless steel. In the center of the morgue, a body covered with a long white sheet lay on a gurney.

Louis breathed deeply, waiting to see Chloe. With all his heart, he wished that this parting could be different. He was relieved that she was dead, but not happy. The idea that he'd driven a tortured soul to suicide would be a heavy weight on his heart for the rest of his life.

In some dim area of his brain, he knew that when the numbness wore off, the guilt would set in. He wasn't free of Chloe, he realized. He never would be.

His wife's mind had been twisted beyond repair. And her rage and anger had known no bounds. He strongly suspected that she had murdered three people. Now she had committed the ultimate act of violent anger—suicide. Unable to bring herself to kill him, she had killed herself instead, knowing that the tragedy would haunt him until the end of his days.

When the older detective pulled back the sheet, Louis's heart stopped. He had expected to see a pale face in a mass of dark curls. Instead, the hair that fanned out on the white sheet was golden.

His breathing became so labored that Louis suspected one of his lungs had spontaneously collapsed.

"Professor Miles, we'd like to ask that you remain in the area until this matter has been thoroughly investigated," one of the men began to drone.

"No," Louis managed to wheeze.

"We really must insist," Detective Farris repeated, mistaking his reaction for a refusal.

Louis shook his head. "No. No. No!" he shouted in a rising panic. "This can't be true. She's not dead."

The detectives seemed to realize that something was wrong. They each took one of his arms. "Professor Miles, perhaps you'd better sit down," Detective Hale said. "Get a doctor," he curtly told his younger partner in a low voice.

Louis savagely shoved both of them away. "Jessica!" he screamed, picking up the body and shaking her. "Jessica! Wake up. Wake up. You can't be dead. Jessica!" he wailed, tears streaming down his cheeks.

Jessica sat straight up when she heard her name. Louis's anguished voice had startled her awake. Her heart raced with fear until she realized that they were still safe in the sun-drenched field. Beside her, Louis thrashed his arms and called her name. But he was sound asleep on the soft grass.

They had dozed off in the peace of the late morning, still exhausted from hours and hours on the road.

She shook him. "Louis. Louis, wake up."

He let out a shout and his eyes opened. When he saw Jessica, he blinked and pulled her down against him. His neck and chest were wet with perspiration and his arms squeezed her so tightly, she feared her ribs would crack. "I had a dream," he said in a tight whisper that sounded more like a sob.

"You had a nightmare," she corrected.

"We have to go," he said.

"Louis. No. I'm happy here. I don't want to leave."

Louis released his grasp and climbed to his feet. Breathing hard, he surveyed the surrounding landscape. "We've got to get out of here."

"Louis!" she cried, standing beside him. "I don't want to go. It was a dream, Louis. A dream. Please," she begged, a sob rising in her own throat. "I'm so scared that . . ." She broke off and began to cry. She couldn't face getting in the car and running again. Here she felt as if they had found a kind of magic circle in which they were safe.

"Please don't make me leave today," she murmured into his chest. "I have a horrible feeling that when we leave, everything is over. And I'm not ready for everything to be over. Let's have today. And tonight. If you still feel the same way tomorrow morning, we'll leave."

She could hear his heart beating hard inside his chest. Slowly it resumed its normal rhythm. He put his arms around her waist and squeezed. "All right," he agreed. "But tomorrow morning we have to go. No arguments."

Elizabeth, Todd, and Gin-Yung stood in the back of the student activities hall watching the enormous monitors. Near the front of the room Dr. Beal and Coach Crane moved among the crowd, smiling and shaking hands.

Sound from the monitors suddenly filled the room, and a good-looking young broadcaster announced the debut of the University Broadcasting System—the first cable channel devoted to NCAA sports.

"And now we're going to go live to Tom Watts of WSVU, the Sweet Valley University TV station. Tom will be interviewing Craig Maser, the Olympic hopeful from California. Over to you, Tom."

In spite of all the friction between them, Elizabeth caught her breath when a close-up of Tom's face appeared on six megascreen monitors around the room. She had almost forgotten how incredibly handsome he was.

His dark hair and eyes lit up the screen. He radiated the same kind of charisma that movie stars did. An intangible quality in Tom's face reached out and grabbed the attention of the audience. There was a hush in the student activities hall, and Elizabeth felt a surge of pride.

"Hello. I'm Tom Watts of station WSVU. I'm here in Las Vegas with Craig Maser."

The camera pulled back to reveal Craig Maser sitting beside Tom.

"Craig," Tom said. "I understand you have something you want to tell our viewing audience."

Craig nodded and cleared his throat. "I want to let the public know that I was approached three weeks ago . . . and offered money to lose this match."

Everyone in the room seemed to suck in their breath with one collective gasp. Elizabeth straightened up and felt Todd clutch her arms.

"When I refused to accept the money, I was threatened. My father is running for Congress. Last year, in the course of a random drug-testing program in the athletics department, I tested positive for illegal steroids. I had a closed-door disciplinary hearing with Coach Crane, head of the SVU athletics department, and Dr. Beal, the director of campus administration. They agreed that if I completed a drug-abuse program and performed fifty hours of community service, there would be no record of the offense. The people who tried to bribe me threatened to make that information public in an effort to disgrace my father if I refused to lose the match."

Craig stopped speaking for a moment. Then he looked directly into the camera. "The only people who had access to those records were Dr. Beal and Coach Crane. I hope that the voters in my dad's district will realize that my bad judgment in no way reflects on his character. In fact, it is because of him and his example that I am making this statement. Speaking the truth is the right thing to do. And I know that it's what he would have done in my place. Thank you, Tom."

"Unbelievable!" Todd yelled, pumping his fist.

The students in the room burst into loud and angry chatter. Dr. Beal and Coach Crane were moving toward the exit doors just as the federal marshals closed in and began making arrests. Elizabeth could practically read their lips as they informed Dr. Beal and Coach Crane of their Miranda rights.

Elizabeth lifted her hands, and Gin-Yung and Todd smacked them with a three-way high-five.

"Still think Tom's not Superman?" Todd teased.

Suddenly something hard pressed into Elizabeth's back. She glanced over her shoulder and saw a tall man. "Don't move. Just come with us."

She threw a glance at Todd. A man stood behind him. From Todd's stiff posture, Elizabeth assumed there was a gun in his back as well.

Gin-Yung darted a look from face to face, then tried to run. But the large man's hand flew out and yanked her back. "Don't make us shoot in here. Somebody innocent might get hurt."

"Since when do you care about hurting innocent people?" Elizabeth spat.

"Come on." The man jerked her arm. "Mr. Santos wants to talk to you."

*   *   *

"Louis," Jessica begged. "Come lie down. We're safe. As long as we're together, what can she do to hurt me?"

Louis stood at the bedroom window, scanning the land around the little farmhouse. A half-moon had risen and the sky was filled with stars. Louis had been edgy ever since his nightmare this afternoon. Throughout dinner, he'd been tense and nervous, unwilling to be separated from Jessica even for a moment.

He paced the floor quietly, dressed only in his khakis. Going back to the window, he peered out for the fifteenth time. The moonlight shone across his bare chest, and his muscles stood out in high relief.

"Tomorrow we're leaving," he said, coming back to the bed. He cradled her in his arms. "I think we'll head for a city. Someplace where we can blend into a crowd."

She put her head on his shoulder. "It's funny that you're the one who wants to go and I'm the one who wants to stay here. I used to like being in crowded cities. I loved all the excitement. Now I like the quiet and solitude." She sighed. "Maybe because there's nobody around to disapprove of us."

"You're thinking about Elizabeth, aren't you?" he asked.

She smiled in the dark. They were getting closer every day, even beginning to read each other's thoughts. She *had* been thinking about her twin. She knew that Elizabeth had a lot of reservations about her relationship with Louis. Well, who wouldn't? She laughed softly to herself.

"What's so funny?"

"I'm just thinking that of all the crazy relationships I've had, this is the craziest—but it's the one that's right for me. No matter what Elizabeth thinks."

He kissed her forehead and smoothed back her hair. "I wish I agreed with you. But I can't think this relationship is right, or fair to anyone. Now sleep," he instructed gently. "I want to leave early."

Louis lay against the pillows with Jessica's head resting against his shoulder. She'd been sleeping for almost an hour now. But he was still awake— and alert to the point of paranoia.

He wasn't superstitious. And he didn't believe in a sixth sense. But he knew that when his nightmares started to haunt him, there was usually a reason. On an unconscious level, some sign triggered his brain to go on overload. The imperceptible scent of rose perfume on a mountain breeze. Or finding a door open just a few inches wider than he had left it.

Whenever his sleep became troubled, he knew that Chloe had found him. He might not know exactly where she was, but he knew she was close.

A creak on the stairs made him catch his

breath. He waited for a second creak, but there was only silence. His eyes cut right and left in the dark. Chloe could move like a cat when she wanted to. She could be in and out of a room or house in minutes without making a sound.

The light in the hallway was on, but underneath the door, he saw it flicker slightly. Was the bulb in the hallway about to go out? Or had someone just walked past the door, disrupting the beam?

Suddenly there was a scent in the air. He sniffed. Was he really smelling roses, or was he smelling the fresh wildflowers that Jessica had arranged on the bureau this afternoon?

Slowly, silently, he removed his arm from beneath Jessica's head and sat up. He put his feet on the floor and began to walk softly toward the door to the hallway. The knob turned easily in his hand. He opened the door a crack and peered out.

Nothing was disturbed. But there was an unmistakable hint of floral odor in the air. He grabbed a white polo shirt from the chair beside the door and shrugged it on. Then he found his jacket with his wallet and keys. He removed two hundred dollars from his wallet and quietly left it on the bedroom's dressing table.

The scent was stronger in the hallway. Louis locked the door to the bedroom behind him, then he slid the key under the door. If something happened to him, he wanted Jessica safely locked inside the bedroom.

Louis crept down the stairs, grimacing every time the wood creaked beneath his feet. At the bottom of the steps he slipped into the loafers he'd left on the landing. In the deep silence, he suddenly heard a faint noise behind the house.

Louis walked through the kitchen and ran an eye over the wooden block that held the kitchen knives. All of them were there—except one. The largest was gone. There was only an empty slot where the butcher knife had been.

Louis swallowed. Chloe was here. And she was armed. He walked out the kitchen door, no longer bothering to keep silent. The trace of rose perfume hung heavy in the air, and he followed the scent to the barn.

He heard a noise inside the barn and he entered, looking around. Except for the moonlight that streamed in through the hayloft, the barn was dark.

Chloe was nowhere to be seen, but the smell of roses was strong enough to choke him. She was in the loft, he guessed.

"Chloe," he said in a voice that was strong and unwavering. "I know you're here. And I'm glad. Because I'm through running away. So come down—let's try to talk this thing through."

There was no answer, but a small hail of dust came raining down from the loft. He turned up his face. "I realize that by constantly drawing away from you, I've just added to your frustration and anger. But what I would like you to understand is

197

that your anger should be directed at me, and at me alone. My friends are not your enemies. Do you understand what I'm telling you?" He stood tensely, waiting for her to spring from the loft with the knife poised.

When she didn't answer, he sighed. "I know I've hurt you. I can never make it all up. But if it means anything at all, I did love you at one time. And I love you still. I will always love you. You're my wife—and if you're willing, we can try again. If you'll come down, we can leave here together. Now. Tonight. We can find a place where no one knows us and start over."

He waited, ready to fight if she came at him with the knife. He was also prepared to embrace her if she accepted his offer. "Chloe. This would be a lot easier if you would say something. I don't know how we can put things back together if . . ." He broke off, realizing that the scent of her perfume was fainter. Louis turned quickly, looking frantically around the barn.

"Chloe," he shouted. "Where are you?"

She was gone, he realized in a flash. And she probably had been from the moment he entered the barn. He ran toward the door. It was closed and latched from the outside. He was locked in.

Louis's eyes finally adjusted to the darkness, and he saw the ladder to the hayloft. He scaled it in a matter of seconds, picked his way carefully across the beams, and climbed out the window.

From the ledge outside, he saw a ladder on the

ground. Chloe had obviously climbed down and then removed it. She'd wanted to trap him inside the barn while she went in the house, where Jessica lay sleeping.

Jessica was locked in, he reminded himself, fighting panic. So he had a few minutes. Carefully he began walking across the roof of the barn. The shingles were flat and slippery. He bent down, using his hands to steady himself, crawling sideways like a crab.

On the other side of the barn was a tree. His foot slid out from beneath him. He momentarily lost his balance, falling down the side of the roof until his fingertips clutched the edge of a shingle.

He pulled himself back up and continued across the roof, finally arriving at the point where a limb reached over the barn. He stepped out on the branch, making his way slowly to the trunk. In the dark he carefully climbed to the lowest limb and then dropped to the ground.

Louis ran around the barn and back to the house. He smelled the odor the minute he opened the back door. Gas.

A high-pitched whistling sound told him that the gas was on full blast—and had been for a while. He ran into the kitchen to turn off the jets of the oven. To his horror, he saw that the knobs had been twisted off. He had no way of stopping the dangerous flow of gas.

The oven was spewing deadly fumes. And so were all of the space heaters, he realized. There

199

were small heating devices in the corner of each room. The air was so thick with gas, he could hardly breathe.

Coughing and choking, he ran toward the stairs, taking them two at a time. He put his hand on the knob of the bedroom door and tried to open it. But it was locked. And the key was inside.

He pounded on the door. "Jessica! Jessica! Wake up. Wake up!"

But there was no answer from inside. The gas had obviously had time to permeate the bedroom. She was unconscious.

He heard Chloe laughing. He didn't know where she was, and he didn't care. He backed up, ran at the door, and broke it down with a splintering crash.

The high-pitched whistling sound changed registers, modulating higher, like a teakettle on full boil. He raced to the bed and gathered up Jessica. Her body was limp and when her head fell backward, her long hair streamed almost to the floor.

Running, he carried her down the stairs. He kicked savagely at the front door. It burst open, and he ran out with Jessica in his arms. He hurtled forward across the yard, finally tripping and falling to the ground. He covered Jessica's body with his own and ducked his head.

Behind him, the explosion shook the ground and reverberated through the mountain canyon like echoing thunder

Chapter Seventeen

Todd got up from wooden bench he'd been sitting on and paced restlessly. "What time is it? I feel like we've been locked up in this basement for days."

Elizabeth looked at her watch. "It's almost ten o'clock."

"So what's going to happen to us?" Gin-Yung asked.

"Maybe we've been entombed down here," Elizabeth said in an ironic voice.

Todd felt a flicker of irritation. "Elizabeth. Sometimes your sense of humor leaves something to be desired."

"Hey! You're the one exhibiting a humor deficit, Todd," she snapped.

"Break it up, you two," Gin-Yung said with a smile.

Elizabeth glowered at her. "We're locked in

Santos's basement. Nobody knows we're here. Somebody's probably going to come kill us. And you're smiling? What's with you?"

Todd returned Gin-Yung's twinkling gaze. He knew why she was smiling. Finally she was convinced that whatever was going on between him and Elizabeth wasn't passion. They had been bickering back and forth with each other for the last two hours. This wasn't the behavior of two people madly in love who were possibly sharing the last hours of their existence.

There was the sound of footsteps, and all three jumped to their feet and stood closer together. The door opened, and moments later Santos appeared with Bobbo and Mark Gathers. Santos and Bobbo both held guns.

Todd met Mark's stare and lifted his lip in a sneer. "Thanks, Gathers. I should have known."

"Shut up," Santos snapped. He looked tired; his expression was hateful. "I don't have a lot of time, so listen up. You kids have cost me a hell of a lot of money and you've put me through no end of trouble. I've been in the DA's office all day, answering questions. I don't like people asking me questions. Tomorrow they're going to arraign Beal and Crane. So here's the question. How much?"

"What do you mean?" Todd asked.

Santos waved his hand impatiently. "How much? How much will it take to get you three to say that Craig Maser is a liar and that the Watts kid put him up to saying what he said to get a story?"

"We're not for sale," Todd said quietly.

"Everybody's for sale," Santos snapped. "Name your price. One million. Two million. It doesn't matter. I can set you kids up for the rest of your lives. Beach houses. Cars. Whatever it is you want." He smiled and his dimples deepened. "I'm your genie in a bottle. This is the best break you kids ever got."

"We're not for sale," Todd repeated, stepping in front of the two girls.

Santos's smile abruptly disappeared, and his eyes snapped dangerously. "OK, then. We'll do this the hard way. Upstairs I've got a family of four. Three of them are very young. Way too young to die." He shook his head in disingenuous sorrow. "But you know what they say. The good die young."

Todd heard Elizabeth and Gin-Yung gasp, but none of them said a word.

"OK, Bobbo. Go get the little boy. Bring him down here."

Bobbo backed up and turned just as Mark Gathers brought his fist up. There was a loud click when Bobbo's bottom teeth collided with his top teeth. The blow stunned him, and he reeled. Todd sprang forward, grabbing Santos's wrist and pointing the gun toward the ceiling. There were two loud shots as the gun fired. Todd and Santos fell to the floor, grappling with the pistol.

Elizabeth and Gin-Yung went for Bobbo. Each

girl managed to get a viselike grip on one of his huge arms. Mark pried the gun from his hand and brought the butt down on Bobbo's head. The bodyguard went down like a sack of potatoes.

Mark ran to help Todd. Together they twisted the gun from Santos's grasp and jumped to their feet. "Gathers," Santos screamed, holding his twisted wrist. "I'll kill you!"

"No, you won't," Mark panted, taking the gun and backing up. "Not unless you can do it from jail. Because that's where you're going."

Todd grinned at Mark and slapped him on the arm. "You did a great job."

Mark grinned back. Finally the four students left the basement, locking Bobbo and Santos in. "Yeah. I did do a good job," Mark said. "If I do say so myself. Daryl and the kids are upstairs locked in the bedrooms. Let's get them out and call the police."

"You mean you're not part of Santos's ring?" Gin-Yung asked as they climbed the stairs to the main part of the house.

Mark shook his head. "Nope. I'm what you'd call an infiltrator. A double agent."

Gin-Yung shook her head sadly. "That's twice today I've been wrong."

Elizabeth smiled. "Mark, if you don't get back into basketball, maybe you could join the drama department. I'd say you gave an Oscar-winning performance as a creep."

*   *   *

"Professor Miles, we'd like to ask that you remain in the area until this matter has been thoroughly investigated."

Louis nodded. "Yes. Of course." This time, the words were real. The policemen were real. The hospital was real. And the nightmare was real.

The explosion had attracted the attention of people from miles around. Within minutes cars had begun arriving. Someone had summoned an ambulance, and Louis had ridden in the back of it with Jessica. They'd gone to the nearest hospital, which was twenty miles away. It was a small, U-shaped building and almost empty. This was not a heavily populated area; the staff and facilities were skeletal.

While the doctor had labored over Jessica in the emergency room, Louis had waited in the front lounge, near the nurses' station. He'd answered the questions of the local police, telling them everything from start to finish.

The police had gone to the farmhouse to investigate, and now they had come back with a report that the explosion had leveled the house.

"You say you heard her laughing inside the house just before you got out?" one of them asked.

Louis nodded. "Yes," he answered impatiently. It was at least the twentieth time they had asked him that same question.

"Professor Miles, if your wife was inside the house, she is undoubtedly dead."

"Did you find her body?" he asked.

"No," the policeman said. "Workers may have to sift through the rubble for days to find conclusive evidence that there was a person in the house when it exploded."

"Then I think you should proceed on the assumption that she's still alive," Louis insisted.

"Professor Miles, be reasonable. We know you've had a shock and this is a terrible trauma, but your wife is no threat to you or anyone else now. What you need is sleep and . . ."

Louis turned away, wondering if he was truly as crazy as they clearly thought he was. All evidence seemed to indicate that Chloe had died in the explosion. But somehow, he just couldn't make himself believe she was gone.

"We'll make arrangements at the motel for you," one of the policemen was saying. His voice went on and on, but Louis wasn't listening. His eyes were glued to the door that led to the emergency room.

The door swung open, and Louis sprang toward the doctor who emerged, looking exhausted. "How is she?" Louis demanded.

The doctor put a hand on Louis's arm. "Relax. She's going to be all right. She's stable."

"Is she conscious?"

The doctor shook his head. "Not yet. But we've moved her to a room. You can see her if you like."

Louis turned to the police. "You need to keep

a twenty-four-hour guard over Ms. Wakefield until we know for certain whether or not my wife is dead. If you won't keep watch, then I will."

"Professor Miles." One of the policemen sighed. "It's been a long night. This isn't New York City, and unfortunately we just don't have the manpower to do that. And it's *not necessary*," he said with gentle emphasis. "I understand that Mrs. Miles has been an ongoing problem. But we're ninety-nine percent certain that she was killed in the explosion. Now, would you like us to drive you to the motel? Maybe once you've had a couple of hours of sleep you'll feel more comfortable."

Louis shook his head. "No, thank you. I'd like to wait and make sure Jessica is all right."

The policeman nodded. "Suit yourself." He handed Miles his car keys. "One of the officers brought your car. When you're ready, drive yourself over to the motel. We'll come get you in the morning and go over the site together. See what we can find. OK?"

Louis nodded and put the keys in his pocket.

"And sir, like we said, please don't leave the area."

Louis turned back to the doctor, who was yawning. "I'll be going home, Professor Miles. A nurse will be on duty at the front desk all night. She has my number at home if there's any problem."

"Where is Jessica's room? Can I see her now?"

The doctor pointed down the hall. "When you get to the end, take a right. It's the last room on the left—near the exit door." The doctor studied him with concern. "Are you going to be all right?"

"I'll be fine," Louis answered, starting down the hall. Or at least he would be fine once he saw Jessica and was satisfied that she was alive and well.

He entered her room quietly. There was a light on, and she was unconscious. Her face was almost as white as the pillow, and her eyes were closed. Louis leaned over and kissed her cheek. Her skin was cool, which disturbed him. He remembered the Jessica in his dream. The one who lay dead in the chilly white morgue. He lifted her hand and held it in his, trying to warm her.

The room seemed to shift slightly, and he realized that he was half-dead himself with fatigue. There was a coffeepot in the waiting room. He'd get a cup and then come back and sit beside her bed.

He left the room and started up the hall. Out of nowhere, a scent assaulted his nostrils. His breathing became shallow, and he turned and ran back down the hall with alarm bells shrieking in his head.

As soon as he threw open the door, he saw her bending over Jessica. The butcher knife was in her hand, the point grazing the hollow of Jessica's neck. The blade was just above the silver unicorn pendant.

Louis dove forward with an enraged shout. Chloe turned, her face looking like an animal's. Her hair was a tangled mass, and her face was painted like a monster's. Her lips were smeared with red lipstick, and her eyes were covered with blue-and-purple makeup that ran to her jawline in horrible streaks. She had never looked more insane than she did now, wearing the makeup she had scavenged from Jessica's stolen kit.

Chloe lifted the knife over her head, preparing to plunge it into Jessica's breast. As the knife came down, Louis dove forward, knocking her to the floor. Chloe was tall and as strong as a man. They rolled over and over as he tried to subdue her. IVs crashed to the floor, while glass shattered as a bedside table overturned.

He reached for her wrist and then groaned at a sudden searing pain in his ribs. His muscles went slack, and he fell back, realizing that the knife was embedded in his right side.

Chloe froze, and her large eyes grew even wider. "No," she whispered.

Struggling, Louis sat up. The knife protruded grotesquely; the pain made it hard to breathe.

"Louis!" she wailed, wringing her hands. "No. Not you. Not you. It's her that I want to die. She's the one I have to kill."

Clenching his teeth, he reached down and grabbed the handle of the knife. Using all his strength, he pulled it from his side. The knife dropped to the floor with a clatter. Blood splattered from the wound, and he clutched at the side of the bed, pulling himself to his feet.

He looked around, but Chloe was gone. He could hear her feet in the hallway, running toward the exit.

Louis sat down in a chair and removed his jacket. He lifted his shirt, examining the wound. Blood seeped from his side. Gritting his teeth against the pain, he went over to the table of supplies and found a thick bandage and tape. Gasping, he taped the heavy gauze to his side, then pulled his shirt back on.

Taking shallow breaths, he went to Jessica's side and bent over her sleeping face. "Chivalry is not dead," he said to her, sobbing with regret, pain, and heartbreak.

He kissed her lips for the last time. "I love you," he whispered in her ear, hoping that some portion of her brain was aware that he was with her. "If you remember nothing else, always remember that."

Quickly, before he changed his mind, he grabbed his coat and his car keys and limped out of the room. He exited the hospital through the back door so that the nurse wouldn't see him. If she noticed his blood-splattered clothes, she would summon the doctor and the police.

"Professor Miles, we'd like to ask that you remain in the area until this matter has been thoroughly investigated."

No. He wasn't remaining in the area. He was leaving. And he was taking Chloe with him.

Louis walked out into the parking lot and stood beside his car for a long time. Just as he expected, Chloe emerged from the shadows, moving toward him with her arms outstretched. Tears streamed down her twisted, horribly painted face. "I never meant to hurt you, Louis. I love you. I've always loved you."

"I know," Louis said, allowing her to put her arms around him and press herself against him. He flinched at the nauseating odor of her perfume.

"I love you," she said, tightening her arms around him.

"We belong together," he said in a constricted voice. Her embrace was causing the searing pain in his side to grow worse. He gently disentangled himself and held her at arm's length. His blood had smeared the side of her dress. But she didn't notice. She was beyond noticing anything. Her eyes were locked on him—in their depths, he saw obsession, despair, and madness. "We belong together," he repeated kindly. "So let's leave before someone tries to stop us."

Chloe gave him a demented smile. "Yes, Louis. Yes. Let's run away. Together."

He unlocked the car and she hurried around to get in.

Louis painfully climbed into the driver's seat and started the engine.

He didn't even bother to knock. The door flew open and suddenly Tom was standing in the middle of the room.

Elizabeth let out a shout of joy and jumped out of bed, throwing herself into his arms. They fell back down on the heap of pillows, and he kissed her so passionately and for so long that she almost forgot the events of the last twenty-four hours.

Several minutes later he drew back his head and smiled at her. "Are we speaking? Or just kissing?"

"Speaking and kissing," she assured him. "Where have you been? I tried to reach you in Las Vegas, but they said you had checked out."

"Are you kidding? Do you have any idea what I've been through?"

"Probably as much as I've been through. Police? FBI? Statements. Statements. And more statements. I didn't leave the police station until six this morning." She looked at the clock and her eyebrows flew up. "Wow! It's nine o'clock. We've got to go!" She pushed against Tom's chest.

"Where do we have to go?" Tom asked, reluctant to release her.

"The ROTC field. Winston and Denise are in the corps, and there's a big drill this morning. We need to go lend our support. Actually it was Jessica's support that Denise wanted. She put a note under the door. I found it when I got home. But I don't want to miss seeing Winston Egbert play soldier."

Tom groaned. "I've been up for twenty-four hours. I sat in the airport for three hours trying to get a standby flight back here, and when I arrive, you want me to go watch Denise and Winston play soldier?"

She wriggled out from underneath him. "Let's take a camcorder," she said. "Maybe we'll get a story."

Tom groaned, stretching out on the bed while she grabbed her shower bag and robe. "I don't know about you, but I've had enough stories for a while," he said.

She laughed and hurried down the hall toward the shower with a light heart. The bad guys were in jail. Tom was back. And everything was turning out just fine.

Elizabeth reached into the shower stall and turned on the hot water. She hoped Jessica would call today. She and Louis could come back now—and let the police worry about his loony wife.

Louis shook his head to clear it. He was seeing double, and he felt weaker and weaker. High, high into the mountains he had driven, looking for just the right place.

The bandage had come off; he'd been bleeding for a long time. The entire front seat was soaked with his blood. Chloe seemed completely unaware of the stain. Completely oblivious to their reality.

Animated and wired, she had alternately chattered happily and raged hysterically as they drove. The edges of his vision were beginning to turn black. He had to act now or never, he realized. He didn't have much time left. Minutes perhaps. Maybe only seconds.

He guided the car to the edge of the mountain road so he could make sure they were high enough. There was no road beneath them—the drop was a thousand feet, at least. At the bottom of the mountain, there was nothing but a rocky canyon.

When the road straightened out and he was sure there was no one in front or behind, he began to accelerate.

Louis drove the car faster and faster as the road began to curve again. Chloe talked on. He had no idea what she was saying. Something delusional and crazy about having to go back and kill Jessica because she was evil and would always come between them.

He purposely didn't look at Chloe. Her face wasn't the one he wanted to carry with him into eternity.

Louis closed his eyes and pictured Jessica—the way she had looked the day he met her in the bookstore. Young. Funny. Sexy. *I love you,* he whispered in his mind. *And chivalry is not dead. I'm doing this to keep you safe.*

He jammed his foot against the gas pedal, pushing it to the floor.

Chapter
Eighteen

"*One* . . . two . . . three . . . four. *Hup* . . . two . . . three . . . four! *March* . . . two . . . three . . . four!" Lieutenant Drake yodeled the count with real military fervor, marching beside the twenty-six-person unit with his chest out and his arms swinging at his sides.

Winston picked up his feet in time with the rest of the company. When the commands came, he halted, turned left, and turned right as if he had been doing these maneuvers all his life. When he heard "about-face," he put one booted toe behind the heel of his other foot and gracefully pivoted one hundred and eighty degrees.

The sun was shining, the sky was a bright blue, and he had never felt more depressed in his life.

He could see Elizabeth and Tom on the sidelines, watching him through dark glasses with smiles on their faces. They weren't the only observers. There were a lot of friends and family.

Most important of all, as Lieutenant Drake had told them over and over, they were being observed by some military higher-ups who were conducting inspections of the ROTC units on campuses all over the country.

"Company, *march*!" Lieutenant Drake screamed.

As one, twenty-six men and women began marching forward in a line. Winston was doing what he could to fulfill his side of the bargain. He was being a man. He had mastered the necessary skills.

But when this inspection was over, he was through. He had filled out his request for a discharge and written a letter to the Freshman Disciplinary Council. He was not cut out for ROTC, and he was fully prepared to leave SVU *and Denise* if they chose to ask him to. The request and letter were in his pocket.

Ahead of him, Denise marched with her gun on her shoulder and her little helmeted head held high. They were marching past the reviewing stand now. "Eyes left!" screamed Lieutenant Drake.

Each soldier turned his or her head toward the stand, craning their neck at that strange angle that Winston had always seen during parades.

Much to his surprise, Denise's head kept turning, until she was marching backward with her head turned in exactly the wrong direction.

"Denise!" he whispered, cutting his eyes in her direction. "You've got it backward."

"You're right, Egbert," she said, giving him a silly grin and crossing her eyes. "I thought Drake was the real man, but the real man was you all along."

"Waters!" Lieutenant Drake yelled in disbelief. "About-face!"

"Oh, sorry, sir," Denise said in a loud voice. Abruptly she turned, swinging her gun carelessly around so that the soldier next to her caught the barrel right in his stomach. "Oomph!" he groaned, bending over and coming to a stop. One by one, the soldiers behind him bumped into each other like a ten-car pileup.

"Company, *halt*!" Lieutenant Drake screamed, running over to them. He began grabbing soldiers, straightening them up and pushing them back into formation. "Get in line!" he bellowed. "What's going on here?"

"Gee, Lieutenant," Denise said in her sweetest voice. "We're trying as hard as we can. I guess Egbert and I are just a couple of weirdo misfits who don't fit in anywhere."

Winston couldn't believe it. His eyes ran over the crowd. Most of them were laughing. But the military brass were shaking their heads in disgust.

"Waters!" Lieutenant Drake screamed, the cords of his neck standing out. "I don't know what you're trying to pull. But this inspection is important to me. So *fall in*."

Denise turned, opened her arms wide, and obediently fell forward against Winston. Her

217

weight knocked him off balance, and he fell, causing the whole unit to fall backward in a ripple effect.

There was a roar of laughter from the crowd.

"Get up!" Drake screamed, almost beside himself with hysteria. "Get up, or you're all dead meat."

Winston somehow managed to get to his feet. He bent over, put his arms beneath Denise's underarms, and pulled her upright. She waggled her head as if she were drunk, then saluted.

"Dead meat reporting for duty, sir!" She straightened up, clicking her heels together. To Winston's delight and horror, she stuck out her tongue and sprayed Drake with a raspberry that was the schoolyard equivalent of a full twenty-one-gun salute.

Drake's beady eyes narrowed, and he started menacingly forward in her direction. Winston immediately stepped in front of Denise. He believed in equality between the sexes. Especially in the military. But he wasn't going to let Drake, or anybody else, bully Denise. "Chill out, Drake," he said evenly.

"Who are you talking to, Egbert?" Drake demanded, shoving his shoulder.

"I'm talking to you, you GI Jerk." Winston dropped his wooden gun and shoved Drake.

The lieutenant came at him with a savage yell of fury. His fists were raised. Winston stood his ground, but before Drake could punch him, most of the unit piled on top of their commander in the biggest group tackle Winston had ever seen.

He stepped back, eyeing the sight with appreciation. Beneath the pack, he could hear a series of guttural grunts and groans that could only be coming from a Neanderthal like Drake.

A small hand tucked itself into his. "Let's get out of here, Egbert," Denise said, her eyes twinkling up at him.

Winston squeezed her hand, and they began walking off the field, leaving the military to solve its own problems. "Denise," he said in a low, caressing voice. "I love you with all my heart. But if you don't stop calling me by my last name, I'm going to sign us both up with the navy."

Laughing, Todd bent down his head and rested it on his arms. Winston had always been funny, but he was beginning to think Denise was even funnier.

"Has Winston always been so hilarious?" Gin-Yung asked in a voice of disbelief.

Todd nodded and put his arm around her shoulders, pulling her against him. Down on the field, some officer types were breaking up the ROTC free-for-all. "He was funny in high school," Todd said. "And he's funny now. But I swear I think Denise might be the true comic genius. Don't ever tell him that, though," Todd said, giving her an intimate smile.

"I won't," she promised, threading her arm

through his. They stood and began walking down the stands. "What happens now?"

Todd whistled. "A lot. We've all given statements." He began to laugh. "I guess in four or five years the case will get to trial. The wheels of justice grind slow, but exceedingly fine."

"Will you get back on the team?" she asked.

Todd shrugged. "I don't know what's in store for me or Mark. At this point, I think we're just content to know that from here on, the athletics program is going to get clean and stay clean." Gin-Yung came to a stop and nervously chewed at a nail. "Something wrong?" he asked.

"You're not mad at me, are you? I mean for getting jealous and butting in."

He laughed. "Would you care?"

She cocked her head to one side. "Yeah. I would."

"No. I'm not mad. And to prove it, I'll take you to lunch. But first I think we'd better drop off Bruce and Lila's keys with a neighbor."

Lila ran to the door when she heard the bell. She hoped to find the deliveryman from Haskin's department store. Lila and her mom had practically bought out the designer section.

Her heart sank when she saw Bruce on the steps. His face looked different. Less genial. He didn't look mad, exactly, but he looked determined. "Lila," he said. "I love you."

Inwardly Lila groaned. He was about to insist

that they get in the car and go home—together. And she didn't want to. On the other hand, she did love him. She didn't want to hurt his feelings.

"But I don't think we're ready to live together."

What? Had she heard him right? "Bruce," she began.

He held up his hand and walked in, brushing past her. "I've given this a lot of thought. I just can't let you sacrifice yourself anymore for me. You're used to the best. You deserve the best. And until I can give you the best, I refuse to let you continue living with me in that cruddy apartment."

Lila smiled, almost giddy with relief. "Oh, Bruce." She sighed, putting her arms around his neck. "What a beautiful thought. I love you so much."

They kissed for a long moment, and he hugged her. "Hey! You're my woman. I've got to look out for you."

Bruce rested his chin on Lila's head and rolled his eyes. He was incredibly relieved. He'd taken a big risk, but his plan had worked. He'd weaseled out of living with Lila and convinced her that he was doing it for her.

She was wearing a silk slip dress, and he could feel her shapely curves beneath the fabric. Lila was a beautiful girl; he truly loved her. But he wasn't ready for a round-the-clock commitment. And unless he missed his guess—neither was she.

*   *   *

Mark saw Alex walking toward the student union. "Alex," he shouted.

She turned. When she saw him, her face clouded over and she quickened her step. Mark ran to catch up and caught at her arm. "Alex, please wait. I want to talk to you."

"What do you want?" she asked coldly, jerking her arm away.

"I wanted to talk to you. To explain what's been going on. And to apologize for . . ." He trailed off and licked his lips. "Well, for *everything*. Look, what you saw in the gym. That was an act. Todd, Elizabeth, and I cooked it up so I could get inside the athletics program and find out what was going on. I'm not the jerk you think I am." He flushed.

She was staring at him, her eyes still narrowed suspiciously. Mark didn't want to give her a chance to tell him off, so he kept babbling. "Well, yes, I was a jerk when I left here months ago and didn't say good-bye. And I'm really, really sorry."

Her expression was skeptical. "You were doing some kind of investigation with Todd and Elizabeth?" she asked.

"Hey! If you don't believe me, you can ask Elizabeth. Or Todd. Or watch the news tonight. The police station was full of reporters last night." He smiled, and she actually smiled back. Except for his fellow investigators, this was the first warm and genuine smile he had seen on anybody's face since he returned.

"I'm dating somebody," she volunteered suddenly.

"The guy in the gym?"

Alex nodded. "Yeah. And I really like him."

Mark felt his heart sink slightly, but he tried to smile and look happy. "What can I say? I've let a lot of good things slip through my fingers in my life. Our relationship is the thing I miss most. But I'm glad you're happy."

She nodded and smiled slightly. He waited for her to turn and walk away, but she didn't. He felt a little flicker of hope. Could her hesitation mean there might be a chance after all?

"I know you're seeing somebody. But could we maybe get together for coffee sometime? I feel like there's a lot I need to tell you. And I'd like to know what's been going on with you while I've been away."

Her fingers twitched nervously at her curls, and she tucked her hair behind her ears. "Are you back to stay?" she asked, not meeting his eyes.

"That sort of depends," he said.

Her eyelashes fluttered down. "On?"

"On whether or not you'll have coffee with me."

Her lips curved in a slow smile, and she lifted her eyes. "I'll have to think about it and let you know."

As Mark watched her shapely figure disappear up the sunny walk, he felt a spark of hope. She hadn't said yes. But she hadn't said no, either.

*   *   *

223

Tom lay on Elizabeth's bed, half asleep. Elizabeth sat at the computer, tapping away at the keypad. She was exhausted, but as she'd said, she was too tired to sleep. So she might as well get started on the copy for the story.

Tom knew he should get up and help her, but he was too tired.

The phone rang, and Elizabeth reached for it immediately. "Hello?" she said quickly.

Tom felt the atmosphere in the room change in an instant. He sat up. Elizabeth sat stiff in her chair, as if she were straining to hear. "Jessica?" she said, her voice tinged with alarm. "What's going on?"

He got up and moved toward the desk. He knew Elizabeth had been worried about Jessica. And from the tension in her voice, he gathered that things weren't going too well. "Where is she?" he whispered.

Elizabeth shook her head. "I can't understand what she's telling me," she whispered. "She's crying too hard."

Chapter
Nineteen

Elizabeth looked out at the ocean. The water was choppy, and the huge, whitecapped waves looked dangerous.

"I'm not sure this is the greatest thing to do," Tom muttered, digging his toes into the sand.

"I think she has to do this," Elizabeth said in a voice choked with tears. She and Tom sat on a large trunk of driftwood a short distance from Louis's beach condo. Elizabeth wanted to stay close enough to be there for Jessica if she was needed, but far enough away to give her some privacy.

Jessica had climbed the stairs to the deck. Now she stood with her face pressed against the plateglass window, looking in. No family had arrived to collect Louis's belongings, and the real estate company had cleared out the condo. Elizabeth had spoken with a representative from the company this morning and found out that it was empty. Louis's things would remain the property of the county for two years. At that time, he would be officially declared intestate. Then, if Jessica wanted some memento of his existence, she could bid on it at a county auction.

Elizabeth had given Jessica the information as gently as she could. But Jessica had still insisted on driving out here for one last look around.

Elizabeth squeezed her eyes closed. The whole situation was cold and inhumane. Louis Miles had fallen a thousand feet into obscurity. Now he was being treated more like a meaningless number than the man Jessica had loved with all her young and giving heart.

A week had passed since Elizabeth and Tom had raced to the airport to meet a weeping and distraught Jessica. Then Jessica had been almost completely silent for two days. Finally, she had been able to tell Elizabeth what had happened—relating the facts between racking sobs. Facts that the police had managed to piece together.

From what Elizabeth knew, it seemed that Chloe had attempted to murder Jessica in the hospital. Louis had tried to stop her, but Chloe had stabbed him, either by mistake or on purpose.

Dripping blood from the room to the parking lot, Louis had led Chloe away from Jessica. Together they had driven into the mountains. Whether or not he had meant to drive the car over the cliff was unclear.

Elizabeth's heart ached for her sister, and she wished she had something comforting to say. But as close as they had always been, she had no words that would comfort Jessica now. There were no words in the world that would ease Jessica's pain. The only thing that would help was time.

"Life is not fair," Tom said under his breath.

"No," Elizabeth agreed grimly, watching Jessica walked down the stairs and out to the water. She took off her shoes and stood still, looking out over the waves while the wind lifted her hair and caused her white sweater to billow around her.

"There are so many happy endings to this story, you'd think there would be one for Jessica," he finished.

Elizabeth swallowed her tears and lifted her face, letting the ocean breeze refresh her. She tried to concentrate on the positives. Daryl Cartright had been offered a fortune for his story by a newspaper. He had also been offered a part-time coaching job at a local junior high. He would be able to move his family into a nicer home, go back to school, and see to it that Lucy got all the medical attention she needed.

Craig's bold confession had inspired public admiration for him *and* his father. Mr. Maser was way ahead in the polls, and after the canceled match Craig had flown to his hometown to campaign for his dad before returning to school.

Elizabeth and Tom had been hailed as heroes,

and UBC had extended job offers to both of them when they graduated. But all of that was a long way off.

Right now, they had to help Jessica cope day to day.

Jessica closed her eyes and listened to the surf. The waves boomed and thundered. Never again would she see or hear the ocean without thinking of Louis Miles.

Tears trickled down her cheeks, and she ached to the very marrow of her bones. Her fingers automatically went to the silver unicorn that hung in the hollow of her throat. The necklace was all she had left to remember him by. That and a rumpled essay on which he had written *A−* and a few critical remarks.

She still couldn't make sense of everything that had happened. She remembered the last few days in bits and pieces. Vivid fragments of heightened reality.

Clear, sharp colors. Gold sunrises. Pink sunsets. Orange cliffs. Emerald-green eyes.

Sounds. The buzzing sound of insects in the warm morning grass. Soft sighs in the dark. Explosions.

Sensations. The flannel of his shirt. The scratchy feel of his beard in the morning. A flutter against her lips.

Had she dreamed it? Or had he bent over her and whispered a final farewell? She liked to think he had. *Chivalry is not dead. I love you. If you re-member nothing else, always remember that.*

Jessica opened her eyes and watched a tall wave rise up, curl, and collapse, disappearing into the vast sea. "Love hurts," she whispered.

Lila Fowler's new boyfriend has secrets—but trying to discover his past may drive her insane. Don't miss Sweet Valley University Thriller #4, **THE HOUSE OF DEATH.** *Lila has never been so scared!*

SIGN UP FOR THE SWEET VALLEY HIGH® FAN CLUB!

Hey, girls! Get all the gossip on Sweet Valley High's® most popular teenagers when you join our fantastic Fan Club! As a member, you'll get all of this really cool stuff:

- Membership Card with your own personal Fan Club ID number
- A Sweet Valley High® Secret Treasure Box
- Sweet Valley High® Stationery
- Official Fan Club Pencil (for secret note writing!)
- Three Bookmarks
- A "Members Only" Door Hanger
- Two Skeins of J. & P. Coats® Embroidery Floss with flower barrette instruction leaflet
- Two editions of *The Oracle* newsletter
- Plus exclusive Sweet Valley High® product offers, special savings, contests, and much more!

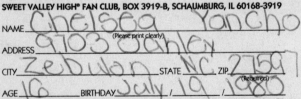

Songs from
the Hit TV Series

SWEET VALLEY HIGH™

Featuring:

"Rose Colored
Glasses"

"Lotion"

"Sweet Valley High
Theme"

**SABAN
RECORDS**™

*Available on CD and Cassette
Wherever Music is Sold.*

Life after high school gets even *Sweeter!*

Francine Pascal's
SWEET VALLEY
SVU
UNIVERSITY
Life after high school gets even sweeter!

Jessica and Elizabeth are now freshmen at Sweet Valley University, where the motto is: Welcome to college — welcome to freedom!

Don't miss any of the books in this fabulous new series.